THE BRUTE

TARRAH ANDERS

Tarrah Anders | Tarrah Anders, LLC

Tarrah.anders@gmail.com |www.tarrahanders.com

Book Formatting: Tarrah Anders, LLC

Cover: BexHarper Designs

Editing, Badassery and Shit: Laura Hull, Red Pen Princess & Indies Ink

Ordering Information:

THE BRUTE | Tarrah Anders.

EBOOK ISBN 978-0-9994426-7-8

PAPERBACK **ISBN-13:978-0999442685**

ISBN-10:0999442686

"Fairy tales are never happy, sweet stories. They're moral stories about overcoming the dark side and the bad."

-- Joe Wright

(Source)

For Maren & Jess.
I love you ladies!

CHAPTER ONE

BENJAMIN

THIS IS THE FIRST TIME THAT MY ASSISTANT IS BEING HIRED without my approval in who will take the position. I chose not to take part in the interview process for my new assistant. It wasn't like the next person would stay longer than the previous one did. So, rather than doing the interview, I assigned someone else who actually gave a fuck, even though the position directly reports to me and supports me. That's not to say I don't care about who works for me; I just don't feel the need to be a part of that process.

I don't have time to meet with candidates who will be not worth my time. It's Human Resources' place to judge character, experience, and skill. After all, it's their job to find the humans I need for my resources.

I run this place. That's *my* job.

I pay someone to do the other shit for me.

I'm halfway through my breakfast and scrolling through some reports that I left on my desk to look over this morning, when the door of my office opens abruptly. The middle-aged woman, head of Human Resources and deposits herself directly in front of my desk with her hands on her hips. Her annoyance is evident in her eyes as I look up at her from the report and my breakfast in front of me. She squares her shoulders, her features looking like she is ready to lecture me and her stance is wide.

Maggie, a woman that I've known since I was a young boy storms in stares me down and clears her throat.

"Ben," she says sternly.

I finger the utensil in my hand and take another forkful of my omelet.

"I would like to introduce to you, your new assistant, Isabella Dubois." Maggie steps aside and reveals the woman I was unaware that was behind her.

I catch a glance at the heavenly sight of her. Rather than allow the strange, ancient feelings simmering in my body to be reflected in my countenance, I feign annoyance.

She has long, chestnut hair, with the ends curled. Almond-shaped eyes over high cheekbones. Shapely lips covered in crimson, the bottom lip a bit plumper than the top. A small, pert nose with a rounded end. Her waist is thin, and her bust is... well, her bust is more than a handful. She's dressed professionally in a white dress shirt and a black pencil skirt. The only bit of color is her turquoise heels, which I'm sure would look great perched on my shoulders as I pound into her while she's laid back on my desk.

I shake my head and rid myself of those thoughts, then return to my breakfast.

I don't need to appraise her on getting the job. Hell, who knows if she will last? I've already gone through five assistants this quarter alone.

What says she'll even survive the week?

"Hello, Mr. Adams." The woman clears her throat and speaks confidently as she strides into my office. She stands in front of my desk, leans over, and holds her hand out boldly.

I look at her hand, but don't take it. She holds it out a moment longer. When she realizes I'm not going to shake her hand, she slowly pulls it back and resumes her ramrod straight posture, then looks at Maggie with uncertainty.

"Ben." Maggie's warning voice comes out.

I look up.

"Welcome to the company," I say with annoyance then go right back to my breakfast and morning reading.

"Isabella has excellent references and experience in handling a... well, a busy environment. I have a feeling that she will succeed and have a lasting term here at Adams Enterprises. I am confident she will excel here."

She wanted to say that this new girl has experience dealing with assholes, because that's what I am.

An asshole.

Everyone knows it; no one pretends otherwise. I don't give a flying fuck about how everyone *feels* about me. Their feelings don't keep Adams Enterprises at the top of its industry. I own this company now and I can fire any of the fools who work here whenever I want.

Except Maggie, she can put me in my place with just a look. When I was younger, and my father was CEO, she worked here in the same position. When I was a kid, she would let me sit in her office and was often a better adult figure than my actual parents were. She's known me almost my entire life. She knew me... before.

This company began as a small family business and my father built it into a titan among its peers. When my parents passed, I was the only heir to the family fortune, including Adams Enterprises. At that point in time, the company had just emerged as a global leader in the tech world. Those who worked under my father remember me as the nice kid who would come and visit his father during school breaks. However, once I took over, they were surprised when I wasn't that person anymore. Loss changes a person. The amount of loss I've experienced made me a different person all together.

Maggie clears her throat and I look at her. Her hands are on her hips again and she tilts her head in the direction of the lovely creature in front of me.

I connect eyes with my new assistant and give her a somewhat genuine smile.

"Glad to have you aboard, Isabella."

CHAPTER TWO

BENJAMIN

YOU'VE GOT TO BE KIDDING ME.

You've got to be fucking *kidding me.*

I look at the schedule Isabella placed on my desk and groan. I lean back in my chair and unbutton the top of my collar and loosen my tie.

I don't want to do anything today except sit in my office and read the mystery novel that popped up on my eReader this morning. It's the latest from a favorite author so I preordered it last month. Yes, I would rather read than meet with any of the simpletons in this goddamn city. Regardless of the amount of pressure that I put myself on with work, I still do my best to find time to read every now and then. It keeps my brain fresh and my tongue sharp.

I have no desire to sit in a room with anyone and have a pissing contest over what the fuck ever they want to talk about. Unfortunately, keep my Fortune 500 company in the top 100, I have to put on a smile and shake hands with the elite of this business world.

"Bella!" I bellow into the empty space of my office.

I can hear the click-clack of her heels as she hurries across the space from her office to mine. She taps on the frame and opens the door, then her lithe body slips inside. She confidently walks across my space and comes to stand in front of my desk.

She's beautiful.

Since she started working for me a few weeks ago, I've noticed other things about her, such as the bright blue color of her eyes that closely resembles Caribbean waters, a smattering of light freckles across her nose, and the small tattoo that lines her wrist under her watch or the bracelets that she wears. I've also catalogued some of her subtle mannerisms such as she purses her lips when she's holding back something she wants to say, or she fiddles with her jewelry when she's concentrating. I can pick up her moods by how her rosy lips situate during her different moods. I am able to differentiate when she's happy, annoyed or biting her tongue in wanting to chastise me. Today, she is wearing a fitted black skirt and a tailored to perfectly fit her shapely breasts sapphire blue blouse. Her shoes, I notice are the same blue as well, matching. It's something she does often: match her shoes and her tops.

"Yes sir?" Her voice is calm, hiding her nerves.

I rattle off a list of things I need from her before any of the meetings this afternoon takes place. Then I instruct her to attend the meetings with me, take notes throughout, and make sure my driver knows what I need this evening after my workout since I have a dinner with Mrs. Anthony afterwards. She takes meticulous notes on the notepad that the brings with her to all of our meetings. She then turns briskly to begin her tasks once it's clear I am finished.

My desk phone chirps, interrupting my not so professional thoughts about my assistant when Bella's soft voice alerts me that the director of purchasing is waiting inside the conference room for my first meeting.

"I'll be there in a minute. Please make sure to send a message to Mrs. Anthony and remind her of our standing reservations this evening."

I laugh to myself. She must think that Mrs. Anthony is my 'Mrs. Robinson', but the truth about her couldn't be more different. I've had a standing dinner with Mrs. Anthony, my late fiancée's mother, once a month for the past ten years. I'm not sure why we still have them anymore since we never talk about her. I shake the thoughts out of my head. *Why do I care?*

A few minutes later, Bella enters the conference room across from my office and shows our colleagues to the medium-sized conference table. I stand and button my jacket before walking over from my office and taking my seat at the head of the table. All eyes are on me as I arrange my notepad and the reports that Bella printed off for the meeting. Bella sits opposite of me at the other end of the table, pen in hand and her attention forward as she waits for me to begin.

I nod my head at her, indicating *go-time*, and I dig into the company's spending and office budgets.

An hour later, everyone leaves the conference room more solemn than they entered, as I cut purchasing spending for the remainder of the year. Bella hangs back and waits until the door clicks closed before she speaks up.

"If you don't mind me saying, sir..." she starts.

"I don't mind," I say to her honestly. In that moment, I realize I don't when she gives it to me straight. This isn't the first time she has voiced her opinion and it certainly isn't the first time I've listened to her with interest. She has a mind for business, which I admire, and I appreciate her thoughts. It's a bit strange though, since I don't allow anyone else to speak to me the way she does.

What is it about her?

"You know, you could move funds around in a lesser department and not cut the purchasing department's budget. They operate at a fuller capacity than some other departments because they supplement everybody." She bends over the table to retrieve scattered papers and pens from the conference room table, alerting my eyes to the movement and opening of her blouse. I can definitely see down her shirt, showcasing her breasts wrapped in black lace. *I'm not completely dead. I notice these things.*

"I could have, but I didn't," I say roughly as I stand, gather my materials, and cross the room to return to my office.

"Ben, you don't always have to be a complete asshole to everyone."

"I meant what I said. The budget is cut for the remainder of the year. I don't want my family's company, my legacy, to fall into the red, ever. We need to spend more wisely. I want a profit increase in each department with a budget and if I have to cut more line items within certain budgets, then I will. I would love it, if you didn't always have to contradict my decisions." The annoyance in my tone is clear.

"You asked me to be always honest with you—," she starts, but I cut her off with a look that says not to cross me.

"Isabella, I would like for you to call Forest Deli and order sandwiches for the lunchtime meeting." I only use her full name to indicate I'm done talking, which she has come to understand in our short time together.

AFTER MY LAST MEETING OF THE DAY, I HEAD STRAIGHT TO the gym. I wrap my hands in tape and step up to the punching bag. Raising my hands into a fighting stance, I toss a few single punches to the bag. I throw a left hook and then step back to switch my stance and do a right roundhouse kick. After twenty minutes of repetitive combinations of punches and kicks, adding in a few more here and there, I'm drenched in sweat. I finish off my workout by jumping on the treadmill and jogging three miles before I towel off and head to the locker room to shower and head to dinner.

Dinner is as it usually is: filled with pleasantries and superficial conversation. Why I continue with these dinners after all these years, I'm not sure. It's not like I was ever really married into the family. It started as a request of Mrs. Anthony after her daughter died. She'd wanted to remain in contact and, at the time, I couldn't tell a grieving mother no. I also couldn't tell her the truth about her daughter. Or the truth that our relationship, our engagement, was crumbling.

The concierge greets me as I approach the elevator to head up to my penthouse. I nod my greeting to him, retreat inside the lift, and wave my access keycard in front of the panel. I watch the floor numbers increase the higher I rise until I finally reach the top floor. My floor.

I walk into my home and breathe deeply for what feels like the first time today. Sure, I've been breathing all day. The average number of breaths a person takes in a day is roughly 23,040. However, I know there are many instances throughout the day when I held my breath. Whether it was on purpose or just a random moment, or whether it was simply because I was around Bella, I'm not entirely sure. But now I feel like I can finally relax and breathe freely.

I approach the bar in the living room and pour myself a glass of Jameson, a taste that I developed for when I was in college and continued into my adulthood. Never wanting to sip on hundred-dollar liquor to show my wealth as I sit in the middle of my couch. The lights are still off, but the moonlight and city lights provide enough glow in the main room to not need a light. I settle into the comfortable sofa, stretch my feet onto the ottoman, and take a light sip. The subtle vanilla flavor hits my tongue, followed by a burst of citrus. Then I swallow, sending a nice burn down my throat. I breathe out and relish in the warmth flowing through my body.

This.

This is what I've needed all day. Two, maybe three, fingers of Jameson while I kick my feet up and not think about a fucking thing. Well, not a fucking thing except Bella.

I shouldn't think of her, and I'm pretty fucking sure she doesn't think of me. Why would she? I'm a bonafide asshole. She probably goes home after work and thinks about anything but me.

But I definitely think of her. How soft her skin must be, how her hair smells, and especially how delectable she would taste. I wonder what sounds would emanate from her throat as I touch her.

I swallow some more of the amber liquid and relish the warmth again as I lean my head back against the couch.

I close my eyes and groan.

I'm fucking horny.

It's been a number of years since I've fucked anyone. And the fact that I'm thinking intimately about my new assistant isn't helping. She works for me, but that doesn't stop me from wanting her. Since it's been years that I've had this desire, I don't want to completely ignore it even though I know one hundred percent that I should. But she gets me. She gets through to me. She's not afraid of me. And yet, I'm completely afraid of her.

I imagine that her skin would be silky and smooth, that her breasts would fit perfectly in my hand, and that her heartbeat would quicken as my hand trails from her knee up to her apex. Her mouth would open slightly as my fingers dance across the edge of her panties and then she would moan softly when I breach her entrance and fuck her with my fingers.

My cock is so painfully hard that I need to let it out of the confines of my slacks. I fist myself and stroke my shaft as I resituate myself in the cushion of the sofa. Imagining having my fingers inside Bella amps up my need. I have to get myself off in order to get my cock under control.

Fuck! The amount of times that I've jacked off thinking about her is innumerable.

I pump vigorously, squeezing and tugging as my hand moves up.

The crown of my cock is sensitive, so I use my other hand to squeeze the tip slightly. I pull my head forward and watch my hands work myself over until come spurts out. Some spills onto my dress shirt and falls around my fist. I use some of my own fluid as lubricant as I stroke the last of my orgasm out of me.

Then I sigh.

I'm almost satisfied.

I would be more satisfied if my cock was experiencing the real thing.

And by that, I mean Bella.

My assistant.

CHAPTER THREE

BENJAMIN

I walk through the building in silence, past cubicles and offices. I notice the employees with their heads down and their eyes forward as I walk by. I know it's because they fear interacting with me or looking at me in a way that I wouldn't like. I've seen that the staff aren't always so enamored with their work when they've thought that I wasn't watching. I also know it's because they are afraid that I will turn to them and fire them for just looking at me, as I've done a few times since I've taken over. At least that's how they perceived the terminations. As long as long the employees do their work and stay out of my way, then I'm happy and they keep their jobs.

Maggie keeps telling me I should be nice to the employees; After all, my father was a well-loved owner. My standard comeback is that I am not my father. He was everybody's friend. I give them paychecks for the work that they do, and they should be happy with that.

I make my way to my office, open up my laptop, and pull up my calendar.

Three months have gone by since Bella was hired as my

assistant. She's lasted longer than any of the others, has done exceptional work with what I've asked of her, can take head on projects with excellence and best of all, she shows no fear when it comes to addressing me, or my moods. In fact, she seems to push through them and even manages to get me to calm down and actually speak to her rather than yell at her. She's masterful in the way she handles me, like that of a football coach, angry but also applauding. She gets me to zero in on her beautiful blue eyes and focus my mind in order to calm down. I think that it's clear that I like her.

We've had many one-on-one meetings wherein previous assistants would have cowered in their seats, perhaps even shed tears.

Not Bella, not a chance. She meets me head on, with the gentlest of touches and the sharpest of fangs.

It could be that most of the time I'm fantasizing about bending her over my desk, or it could be that I'm in complete awe of her. I'm not sure, nor do I care. She gets the job done, does it well, and so far hasn't made me look like a complete idiot in any of my business dealings.

Maggie waltzes into my office with the confidence and swagger of a panther. She never bothers to knock and, while that annoys the shit out of me with others, I cannot bring myself to getting angry at her for doing so. She tosses several folders down onto my desk in front of me. The whoosh of air from the files landing with such force makes me blink. I look down at the files and then back up to her with a quirk of my eyebrow.

"The top file is the employee file on Isabella. Her three-month evaluation is due and, as her boss, you are required to meet with her. Are you satisfied with her performance?"

Her performance would better if she pleased me the way she does in my fantasies.

"Her performance has been stellar," I respond, my tone practiced and even.

"Good. She seems to get along with the vendors and staff. And most importantly, with you. She seems to be thick-skinned and not inclined to hide in a corner with her tail between her legs," Maggie praises. "She's outlasted the others."

I nod. "I've noticed that as well."

"Any specific reason she hasn't come to my office in tears because you're being an untamed animal?"

"The others were incompetent. They were scared puppies with their tails between their legs as you just said. I was no different with them than I am with Bella. She goes toe-to-toe with me."

"And you don't mind that?"

"Irrelevant. Honestly, her input has been helpful in some instances. Don't worry. I'll get the review done. Anything else, Maggie?"

"No. And good. If you could please have it finished by the end of the week. I would like the file back on my desk by close of business on Friday. Can you do that?"

"Yes ma'am." Maggie scares me sometimes with her mean expressions and her overall authority that I remember from my childhood. No chance in hell I would ever cross her in a dark alley, but I also would rather not prolong conversations with her. She thinks that just because she's known me since before I could drive, that she knows me still as that person today.

As Maggie leaves my office, Bella enters. She crosses the room and takes a seat in front of my desk with her notepad and pen. She's poised and ready to take her morning notes, which I prefer to do in person with her rather than through an email like I did before her. Her pen hovers over the paper and her eyes are fixed on me, awaiting my start.

I watch her as she sits patiently with her legs crossed. She's always ready to jot her notes down, always attentive.

"Today, we're going to discuss you," I say finally, leaning back in my seat.

"Me?" she asks, pointing her pen at her chest. *That chest... mmmm. Yes, I would like to talk about your breasts.*

"That's correct. You. You and me," I reply, watching her expression carefully.

Her skin flushes. From under her blouse, the blush rises up her neck to her face and the tips of her ears get the brightest. I note by the vein on her slender neck that her pulse has quickened. Her breathing has increased. I notice the change, satisfied that I can create this effect within her with just my proximity and my words.

She clears her throat. "What about you and me?" she asks.

I stand, button my jacket, and round the massive oak desk that separates us to stand directly in front of her in the limited space between the chair where she sits and my desk. I cross one foot over the other and lean back on the desk. Her face is in perfect range to suck me off if she happened to lean forward a foot, but I shake my head to clear those thoughts. I'm her boss, I'm asserting myself as her boss, so I need to keep my cock in check. Although, as I look down at her, she licks her bottom lip, glances in the general direction of my cock, then back up to meet my eyes.

"You and me, Bella. Me and you. What do you think?" I ask gruffly, hinting at my true intentions but without blatantly stating them.

"I'm not exactly sure that I know what you're asking, sir." Her voice conveys confidence, but she begins twisting the stud in her left earlobe.

"You have become a passionate and dedicated employee and it's time for your three-month evaluation. I would like to know how you feel about working here and your position with me." I ask.

She shifts subtly in her chair. I enjoy watching her squirm, knowing that I have some effect on her. Her eyes dart down to her lap, then she blows out a breath and looks up to meet my eyes again. I'm still picturing her rosy red lips wrapped around my cock when she answers.

"I enjoy working for you. I've learned so much about the industry, and I feel like I've been doing my job with accuracy and efficiency."

"I'm a difficult person to work for, although you've seemed to be able to handle my moods. Is that a problem for you? My difficulty?"

"I don't think you're difficult. I think you are misunderstood."

"Misunderstood?" I question. "Explain."

"I think that you can be standoffish. Although, you don't seem to be around me. But I see how you care about this company, how you love what you do. I also see that you have a general interest in the staff around here, even though you're an asshole at times and no one else sees it."

"An asshole?" I fake astonishment, as if I've never overheard employees describe me that way. Hell, I've always personally acknowledged being one.

"You want me to be honest?" She asks for permission. *Cute.*

When I nod she continues. "Well, you aren't the nicest person around. You can be short with others, are occasionally heartless, and you frequently make it clear that it's your way or the highway. I get it though; this company is all you have. I would want the best for my brand if I were in your shoes. But you sometimes yell at the staff, and you often don't offer an explanation for your behavior or your decisions, so you have this reputation."

I know the reputation she speaks of. This isn't the first time it's been brought up.

"And you're okay working for an asshole?"

"You aren't an asshole to me."

"No?"

"I mean, you have your moments, but underneath it all I know you genuinely care for everyone here. I feel like I can get through to you, or at least meet you halfway."

"So, you're calling yourself an asshole as well?" I smirk.

"I have those tendencies, I suppose." she shrugs.

I laugh lightly and shake my head as I stand to my full height and take the seat beside her.

"I don't believe that for one second," I say, my voice just above a whisper.

She looks at me and I can see it in her eyes. She is curious about me, and she's definitely attracted to me. I can see the tell-tale signs.

"The gala on Friday night. You're attending, as my date," I state as I stand and return to my chair behind the desk. I move the files that Maggie brought in to the side of my desk and fold my hands in front of me.

"Your date, sir?" she asks, confused. "I wasn't planning to attend the gala. I can't. I don't have a dress. I haven't scheduled an appointment to have my hair done, my makeup, a pedicure..." Her voice trails off as she stares absently at the side wall with worry. Though she spoke her thoughts out loud, they likely they weren't meant for me.

"Those are not valid reasons for you to say no. I have people who will take care of all that for you and I will have a car pick you up at six."

"Sir, I'm a little confused. From what I've seen in the press, you usually already have someone lined up to take with you to these events. Why me?" she asks, standing.

She's right. In the past, I have always hired a stand-in escort to attend events with me. It seemed the best solution to have someone who wouldn't ask for more time or emotion than I would care to give, someone I could trust to be discreet, and someone who would be *available* to me if I so choose. I've never indulged in that benefit of the agreement, but the option was always there. I'd just needed someone who knew her duty was to smile and be present, so I wasn't presented to the public as a complete recluse. Because, even though I do keep myself isolated, I need to maintain appearances for the benefit of my company. Sometimes those *appearances* include the image that I have a personal life.

"Because I would rather that you attend," I reply honestly.

"But why?" she prods.

"Isabella. Do I need a reason to take a beautiful woman anywhere?" I ask her, knowing that this is no way professional of me.

"No, sir. I'm just wondering, why me? I've seen pictures of the women you've attend these things with in the past. They are very striking women."

"Because I would be honored to take you as my date. *You* are very striking and I think that we would make a good team to best represent Adams Enterprises at the event. Although, it's a night of fun and not of work."

After a moment of hesitation, she asks, "Is my attendance part of my review, sir?"

"Not at all. I consider your review complete. But I do hope for your company."

She blushes, looks at her feet and then as she looks up with a tentative smile.

"As long as my attendance does not interfere with my employment and it's just a night of enjoyment," she replies.

"Good." I switch gears. "Now that all of that is done and

settled, I have a few requests for this week and the meetings that are planned." We continue talking about the business side of things for the remainder of the hour, even though I would much rather discuss the gala and what could happen afterwards or – hell – even during.

As the day wears on, I pass Bella's desk several times. Each time, I catch her curious eyes on me as I either walk to or from my office. Her smile is innocent, but also hides a secret. A few times I noticed her blush as she resumed her work. I feel like we have shared something, something deeper than boss and employee, and I hope that she feels the same.

This is going to be a long week.

CHAPTER FOUR

BENJAMIN

Friday couldn't have come soon enough.

I am eager to see Bella dressed in a gown, to have her on my arm, standing close to me, laughing with me, touching me.

I scowl. *This isn't me. I'm not this person.*

I arranged for a personal shopper and a stylist to tend to Bella this evening. I also gave her the afternoon off while I spent my day working from home. At the appointed time, I dress in my tuxedo and sit down to wait for Bella. The car I sent to pick her up was headed here to my home so we could leave for the gala together.

I'm sitting in my library, reading a thriller novel to avoid thoughts of anything but this evening, when the elevator chimes rescuing me from my attempts to keep distracted. When I hear that melodic sound, I toss my book aside and jump up to go greet my guest. I dash out of the library and into the hallway, buttoning my jacket as I go. Bella rounds the same corner while my eyes are looking down at my fingers working the buttons. Mrs. Rosemary, my cook and household manager, must have greeted Bella at the elevator and directed my guest to the library.

We crash into one another with an "oomph" and my hands reach out to steady her. I feel the magnetic pull of our bodies touching; it was brief, but it was there. I haven't felt that zing in years, not since before everything happened in my last relationship with *her*.

"I'm sorry. The lady directed me in here," she apologizes as she looks around. "I feel so weird being in your personal space."

I would prefer she was a lot closer to my personal space.

"It's cool. I was actually coming out to greet you," I reply.

"Cool? You said *cool*," she snickers.

"What? I'm human, you know," I remind her.

"I know. It's just that, in the office, you're so to the point. No hip lingo. None of those everyday things you hear others say. You're all *businessy*."

"Isabella, I don't believe *businessy* is a real word," I tease.

Her eyes focus on something over my shoulder and widen. She pushes past me and stops in the center of the room, then turns her body so she gets a 360-degree view.

"What is this?" she whispers.

I walk to stand beside her and smile, my hands in my pockets.

"This is my library. it's one of my favorite places in my home."

"You read?"

"I've been told by previous professors that I have a skill for reading."

"I'm sorry. What I meant is, *you* read?" She changes her tone slightly.

"I like to keep my brain fresh, so yes, I am an avid reader."

"How many books are in here?" She motions around the room.

"Thousands. I'm not sure. I've never taken the tally. I take it you like books?" I ask her.

"Extremely. If I were home right now, my head would be between the pages of a book, or I would be swiping through pages on my eReader. I'm an equal-opportunity reader. As long as I'm reading, I'm happy."

"Noted. Anyway, shall we go? I hate to pull you away from what may seem like your own personal heaven, but you can explore in here later."

"Later?" she asks, as I put my hand on her elbow and escort her to the elevator. I ignore her inquiry and the questions in her eyes.

I DIDN'T TAKE THE TIME TO APPRECIATE PROPERLY HOW marvelous Bella looks until we're standing in the press line to enter into the gala. Of course, this gala is Hollybrooke's single most important event of the year and the who's who of the city is in attendance tonight.

Bella is a vision in a burgundy-colored gown embellished with black beads in a floral pattern that glisten when they catch the light and when the embellishments end at her hips, the dress calls attention to her elegant figure every time she moves. The lower part of her dress from her mid-thighs down to her toes is black satin with a slit up her right side showing off her long, shapely leg. The keyhole back showcases her soft ivory skin and shows a hint of a hidden tattoo. The bust is modest with a heavy amount of the embellished beads angling towards her bust and disbursing more evenly towards her waist. I see the goosebumps rise on her forearms from the sudden contact with me and wrap my arm around her waist.

"Don't be afraid of the cameras and the lights. Just smile and follow what I do. You'll be great. You look breathtaking, by the way," I whisper to her as we approach the photographers. She smells heavenly, like flowers in the breeze, as my nose lightly brushes against her hair as I speak softly into her ear.

She fits perfectly under my arm, and she doesn't seem to be taken aback by my move to hold her close. We've approached our turn and we pose for the cameras and the parade of questions that are generally asked of everyone.

"Benjamin! Benjamin! Mr. Adams, over here! Who is your date? How long have you two been together? Who are you wearing? What's next for you?"

We turn from camera to camera and smile for several minutes before going on our way. At the end of the red carpet, my arm is still around her. I shift and take her elbow to help her balance as we head up the stairs together, then through the double doors that open as we approach.

At the top of the stairs, I move my hand back around her waist and squeeze her hip. Pulling her close to me, I place my mouth close to her ear. "You did fabulously," I whisper to her as we walk through the doors. Seeing the simple words make her smile and the goosebumps rise on her skin makes me elated.

The ballroom is lavish in its decor, done in tones of oranges and pinks, with silver accents. People are everywhere. Some guests are dancing in the center of the room, while others chat around tables scattered throughout the space or mingle in the open spaces. Servers zig-zag in-between guests with trays of champagne and platters of hors d'oeuvres.

I recognize several people with whom I do business, as well as a few acquaintances. I see Henry Matthews, one of my only friends, and I make a mental note to speak with him at some point this evening. He's standing with a few women who, by the looks on their faces, are quite charmed by him. He catches my eye and holds up his glass in my direction and we nod to ONE another. I move Bella through the room and towards the bar area.

"Shall we?" I motion my hand towards the open bar area.

"Please?" she requests.

"Nervous?" I ask as we wait in line.

"I've just never been to an event this fancy. I'm not sure exactly how to act or stand, or anything."

I laugh lightly. "You are doing a great job. Remember to relax; this evening is about fun. You're not here working."

"But you're my boss."

"No, Isabella, I'm your date for the evening," I say.

"Whatever you say," she rolls her eyes as we step up to the bar.

Once we get our glasses of wine, I'm approached by a few heavy hitters in the industry and get sucked into conversation. With my arm still wrapped around Bella's waist, we talk about business, even against my wishes that tonight not be about work. Bella interjects with confidence when I stumble a few times trying to recall my schedule and helps me not look like a complete fool. She fends off a meeting for me and excels at holding her own. She smiles and shakes hands with the men as well as the women. While I'm speaking with one of my associates, she maintains a conversation with his wife. I lean closer to her and try to listen in on her conversation once the gentlemen in front of me have begun speaking to ONE another, and I've grown bored with their chatter over some unimportant ventures of theirs. Bella is talking books and small towns with one of the wives and I wonder how they arrived on that subject. When their conversation seems to stall, I steer Bella away and towards the dance floor.

"I don't dance," she whispers to me as if we're conspiring together.

"That's okay, just follow my lead."

"Mr. Adams, I didn't take you for a partygoer who enjoys dancing," she says with a light laugh.

"Oh, Isabella, I'm not, normally. But tonight, I feel like showing off my lovely date."

Without giving her more time to refuse, I take her hand in mine, spin her out, and then pull her back into my body. She almost crashes against me but manages to right herself on her feet quickly. My right hand is on her lower back, just above her ass, and my left holds her hand out to the side. She looks at our feet between our bodies as I move us around the floor.

"Eyes up here," I instruct her.

"Is this where you tell me that this is my dance space and that is yours?" She smirks.

"This is where I get your undivided attention." I smile, thinking she's cute for referring to the 1980's cult classic, *Dirty Dancing*.

She cocks her head and studies me, as if all her questions might be answered by observing me.

"You're acting different. Why?"

"I'm acting the way I normally act with you," I reply simply.

"No, you're acting… different. Softer. I'm not really sure, but it's definitely not the usual you."

"We're not at work; we're enjoying an evening out," I reply.

"C'mon, Ben. You ask me to give it to you straight, so I'm asking the same in return."

I sigh, press my chin to her temple and pull her closer as I turn her in time with the music. "I'm tired."

"Oh, if you're tired, we don't have to stay. You can have the car drop me off." She tries to pull away but my grip on her is tight and I won't let her interrupt our dance.

"I'm not tired in the sense of being exhausted." I pull my head back and look at her beautiful face. Her eyes are full of curiosity.

"Then I'm confused." She shakes her head, and looks into my eyes to try to decipher my thoughts.

"I'm *tired* of avoiding my feelings, my thoughts, about you in the way that I want. I'm tired of pushing aside my desire for you."

"Wait, what?" She angles her head, her eyes curious.

"You," I say quietly, leaning into her.

"Oh." She's surprised.

"Isabella, I've wanted you since you first walked into my office and tried to shake my hand. I've wanted you every day I've known you. No one talks to me the way you talk to me, and I don't talk to anyone the way I talk to you. *You* are my desire. I'm tired of hiding that from you. I want you, that's what I mean. I've held back and kept my mouth shut, but I'm finding that I can't any longer."

"Ben, I'm not sure it's wise to mix business with pleasure, especially since you have the power to fire me. Or because it would look bad with the other staff."

"I respect that and I don't want you to feel uncomfortable. I mean, I'm sure if you don't return the same feelings, this can be really awkward." *Shit, did I just mess this up?* "I don't want you to do or say something that you might regret. But I urge you to consider the possibilities. Business and pleasure can be two separate things. Besides, I have no reason to fire you; you're the best assistant I've ever had. If you want me to forget this, then I will, but believe me when I say that I don't want to," I say quietly.

"You're my boss, Ben. There's probably something forbidding fraternization in the employee handbook."

"There isn't."

"Ben," she says in a warning tone.

"Bella," I retort. "Just consider it."

"You're an HR nightmare." She laughs.

"Does that mean you'll consider it?" I ask with hope.

She smiles and leans her head on my chest as we continue to dance.

I'll take that as a *yes*.

CHAPTER FIVE

BELLA

Since I started working at Adams Enterprises three months ago, I put my social life on hold. This job has become important to me for some reason and, strangely, *he* has become important to me as well. He's my boss and he shouldn't be important to me on a personal level, but there's just something about him that draws me in.

He can be a complete animal and everyone warned me from the moment I started at Adams Enterprises. However, he's different with me. He's softer, he listens and he genuinely seems to care. Yes, I've seen him single-handily fire an employee – likely for looking at him – but overall, he's misunderstood.

I came to Hollybrooke for a change of scenery. I was the quintessential small town, farmer's daughter seeking adventure in the big bad city, the girl who always stuck out in the small community where I grew up, some two hundred miles from here. I grew up learning the ropes of farm life with my older, and much more country-fied brother. My father intended on the both of us looking after it once he was gone, but I had different ambitions in life. My ambitions didn't include tilling the soil, feeding the hogs, or picking the fruits adorning the trees that filled half our property. I worked for a few businesses back home after school, so I had office experience and some experience in dealing with high powered men, or as high powered as one can be in our small town. I left few months ago to seek this adventure, not knowing what I was looking for until I set foot in Benjamin Adams' office and held out my hand to him.

The shock of Ben asking me to accompany him to the gala took some time to soak in. I was hesitant to go, in fear that my job would be in jeopardy if I did go by the publicity that would likely come from the two of us stepping foot outside the office together. But then I thought about it a little more while he was making his arguments and I figured maybe I should live a little. Going to the gala could be part of my adventure.

So, I went, and it was a grand affair. I've read about galas in books and now I can say I've been to one. From the blinding lights of the press when we arrived, to the conversations with the wives of Ben's associates, to the dancing in the glamorous ballroom, it was an overall grand evening. The most surprising thing of all was Ben's confession.

Since meeting him, I have fought against having any inkling of feelings for him. But then he broke the dam. Suddenly, he was all I could think about.

Dancing with him at the gala felt like a scene from a movie, with his strong arms holding me, and his confident frame leading me around the dancefloor with ease. He made me feel graceful in his arms. He made me feel cherish, with his silky, yet raspy, voice as he tells me how he feels about me and yet gives me the choice to accept or decline his offer. To decline him. The way that he brushed stray hairs off of my forehead at the end of the night when his driver dropped me off at home and squeezed my hand as he leads to me my door. He stayed a true gentleman and kissed my hand rather than pressing me against the door when he dropped me off, which, honestly, I wanted more than anything deep down in my gut. I want him. This I know. But can I toss out everything that I was taught in regards to professional life and personal life being separate?

As I was getting ready for bed, he sent me a text saying that he enjoyed the evening and to have a good weekend.

A good weekend?

How am I supposed to have a good weekend when my mind is racing as if it's on the Autobahn and I'm picturing my boss naked?

I'M SITTING AT A CAFÉ CLOSE TO MY HOME WITH MY FRIEND and neighbor Felipe on Sunday afternoon. I've dished about my concerns regarding what Ben has proposed and described everything from Friday night in detail. I sip my cappuccino as he looks up at the ceiling in deep thought.

"Oh, mija," he starts, exaggerating his Latin accent for dramatic effect, while leaning forward as if we're planning a bank heist. "Don't you know you need to live a little? I mean a little dick, even boss dick can do someone good. It sounds to me mija, that he's willing to overlook the hierarchy here if you are."

I smile at Felipe and his deep-seated belief that everyone should live big and ignore all naysayers, and lean back in my chair.

"This is my first real-world job in a big city, I'm not working for my dad shoveling hay on my family's property. I may be naïve in some areas, but wouldn't getting involved with my boss be an issue?" I ask, setting my cup down and fiddling with the handle.

"Not if boss-man isn't," he tsks.

"That's horrible advice," I snicker. "He's a guy and could very well just want to get laid," I add with disdain.

"Then he wouldn't be risking getting involved with you. Listen, mija, I've seen pictures of your boss; he's a looker. And he's rich and powerful. If he wants to snap his fingers and have someone *service* him, he certainly can," he says, as I make a face. "Sorry, mija, it's the truth. But it seems he would rather have *you* service him."

I wad up my napkin up and throw it at him. "You're not helping," I say with a giggle.

"I'm a guy. I'm giving you a guy's point of view." He smiles.

"You're a guy who dates guys," I retort.

"Like there's a difference." He rolls his eyes.

"So, what you're saying is that I should do it?"

"If by *it* you mean the horizontal mambo, going to pound town, spray painting the cervix, loading the clown into the cannon, then fuck yes. Wait, no he looks like a strong powerful man. You'll definitely get nailed to the wall."

"Well, thanks for adding that to my imagination." I groan. *Not like it isn't an intriguing thought. Nope, not at all.*

"That's what I'm here for."

THE BEGINNING OF THE WEEK, BEN IS OUT OF THE OFFICE. He's gone to the coast looking at developments. We communicate a few times a day about work matters. Ben doesn't bring up his proposal and I don't either, which gives us a few more days of avoidance. I have thought long and hard about the pros and cons of getting involved with him and maybe Felipe was right. Ben wouldn't take the risk if it was just a fleeting moment of carnal weakness. There must be more to his attraction.

CHAPTER SIX

BENJAMIN

I'm out of the office for the first half of the week, traveling to the coast to look at some real estate for a new office location for an expanding division of Adams Enterprises. Even though the trip was a let-down because I found nothing particularly to my liking, I did stay at a lovely hotel overlooking the ocean and took time to do absolutely nothing, which I've never done.

Doing nothing proved dangerous, however. It left me with thoughts of the past, depressing thoughts that I've hidden for years by keeping busy.

Nine and a half years ago, I was twenty-four and had just graduated college during the winter ceremonies with a business degree and a minor in electrical engineering. I was set to start a new company with my college-friend Elliot, when I was called home because my parents were in an accident. My parents were at a ski resort on their anniversary, when the cable line on the ski lift they were riding suddenly snapped and they plummeted to the ground. They were killed instantly when part of the apparatus landed on top of them. It was a freak accident.

In an instant, I went from an excited college graduate to a mourning son and family business heir. My father's will had specified that I would inherit his technology business and I would sit at the head of the table. I tried to argue with his lawyers and get stockholders or a board to take it over, but the instructions were ironclad, so I had to abandon my start-up with Elliot.

I dove in right away, trying to learn the business. Even though I grew up in the company, I had a lot to learn. At that time, I hated life, I hated the company, and I definitely hated that I suddenly had all this responsibility I didn't ask for. Running the company provided a constant reminder that my father was gone and my life was no longer what I wanted it to be. As a result, I acted like an entitled child.

I was prevented from starting up the dot-com company with Elliot as we had planned. Instead, I had mergers to broker, I had new ideas to cultivate, and I had to learn my father's business all over again. While I understand technology and the way that electrical components play a part, standing at the helm and steering the company was a whole new set of skills I had to learn. Adams Enterprises was not just a creator of home systems, of all things home technology, it had become a nation-wide leader in several tech fields. I took night classes to expand my business management knowledge and I eventually became the leader I needed to be. But in time I became a different person.

Renae – my college sweetheart-turned-fiancée – did what she could to encourage me and keep my spirits up. But as hard as she tried to get my attention, I closed myself off to her. I was an only child, my parents and I were close, and I'd spent my summers interning at Adams Enterprises. Everything felt tinted by the loss; my world was ruined.

I don't blame Renae for what she did. We were young, and I

ignored her. I took the emotional support that she offered me and gave her nothing in return. Looking back, I see that things should have just ended before she chose to cheat on me, but I give her credit for not wanting to add one more heartbreak to my plate. After all, I only became aware of her cheating on me after she died a year later in a car accident.

WHEN I RETURN TO WORK, I HAVE NO EXTRA PEP IN MY step. When I walk through the building lobby and into the elevator, I am sure as hell am not cheery and recharged, as one should be after staying in a beachside hotel for three days.

I ignore all the people in my path and walk straight into my office, even ignoring Bella, who promptly gathers a pen and notepad and follows me into my office. She waits silently as I remove my coat and place it on the coat hook behind my desk. I turn around and unhook my cufflinks and roll up the sleeves of my dress shirt to the elbow, showcasing the lower portion of my sleeves of tattoos. I sit down, bring my computer to life, and fold my hands together in front of me on the desk.

Bella's eyes widen at my colorful forearms on display for her and it hits me that she didn't know that I have tattoos. It's a fact about me that no one at the company knows, a personal expression that I don't share with employees.

"So colorful. I wouldn't have expected you to have tattoos," she says.

"Most of them I got before... well before I took over the company. Some of the elements I got in more recently." I catch myself before I share too much.

"They're beautiful," she whispers, looking away. "You're beautiful," she mumbles to herself.

"So, what do we have today?" I ask, tapping my hand on the desk and wanting to change the subject.

Right as Bella opens her mouth to respond, Maggie bursts into the office, eyeing both of us suspiciously. She regards Bella with a simple nod and then focuses all her attention on me.

"Ben, a word? In private," she says slowly.

"Bella, would you please excuse us? I'll call for you when I'm ready to figure out the remainder of the week," I say evenly. I'm annoyed by Maggie's interruption; no need to take it out on Bella.

Maggie watches Bella leave my office and then walks to the door and closes it.

"Benjamin Adams," she starts. Not a good sign when she uses my full name. "Is there something going on between you and Isabella?"

My tone reveals my annoyance when I reply, "What the hell would give you that impression? The fact that she's taking notes like she does every day in my office?"

"You took her to the Hollybrooke Gala," she replies, aghast.

"And? Last year I took a hooker." I roll my eyes and sit back in my chair. "So what?"

"You do realize that this could be considered taking advantage of your authority over her? She's your direct employee. It could become a lawsuit against Adams Enterprises."

"I invited Isabella as my guest because I failed to make preparations and secure a *date* ahead of time. The fact that Isabella came with me to the event is inconsequential. Also, if we were to become involved, I can promise you that it would be no one's business but ours, and would have no effect on the Adams Enterprises landscape."

"I would like to update the company handbook. In the wake of this occurrence, I realized that we do not have a section regarding staff fraternization and I think it is imperative to add one."

"Maggie. Everyone on my staff is an adult. I do not wish to infringe on their social lives."

"Leaving this open poses a potential problem, Ben. It leaves us wide open in the instance that something occurs. You know this. Think about it. What if—"

"Maggie, there is no *what if*. Leave it be. I do not wish to add any additional rules to the handbook at this time and that's final."

"But—" she starts.

"My father didn't see a need, and neither do I," I respond, a bit frustrated.

"Ben. You know as well as I do that the workplace atmosphere is a difficult place than it was when your father ran the company. Thousands of harassment complaints are made daily regarding incidents in the workplace. I want to avoid that becoming a problem here."

"I don't think anyone here has to worry about me harassing them." I laugh. "Everyone here thinks I'm an ass."

"It could be another staff member," she retorts.

"It could be, but I would rather trust in my employees not to be fucktards."

"Can we at least have a harassment prevention seminar? That way the staff knows what is and is not appropriate and how to report such things?" Her frustration is clear in her tone.

"By all means." I wave her off, hoping she will leave now that I've agreed to at least one thing.

"And Isabella? There is nothing going on between the two of you?" She hesitates by the door, one hand on the handle.

"Correct," I say through clenched teeth. I'm irritated at Maggie's haranguing, but I'm also wishing that I was lying, that there was something happening. I felt our connection when we danced, when I told her how I felt. She returns my feelings, she was just suggesting that we not pursue them due to our circumstances. Even though that I could tell that as the night wore on, that what I had said was waffling in her decision.

Maggie leaves my office and I ask Bella to return. She walks in, clearly nervous.

"Everything okay?" she asks nervously. I nod, not wanting to discuss what Maggie had said.

She rattles off what I've missed so far this week, along with what's on my schedule for the rest of the week. Once she's finished, I request some needed tasks from her, then she stands to leave the room. She stops in the middle of the room and turns.

"I, umm, had a good time on Friday night at the gala. Thank you for taking me." She smiles hesitantly.

"As did I. Thank you for being my date." I nod and smile.

"There are photos of us. On the internet. I don't think I've seen you smile like that before," she says, her eyes catching mine.

"Must have been the company I was with."

She turns and heads towards the door.

"Oh yeah, Ben?" she calls from the doorway, her voice confident.

I look up, quirk my eyebrow in question and wait for her to continue.

"I've reconsidered." And with that she's gone.

She's knocked the wind out of me.

I DID MY BEST TO CONCENTRATE ON MY SCHEDULED meetings and tasks, but my thoughts were consumed by Bella and her declaration. While I was not expecting her to change her mind, I'm rather pleased that she did. Several times throughout the day, I had a free moment and would attempt to talk to her, but she was either on the phone or away from her desk. By the end of the day, I was so engrossed in work and trying to play catch up, that I failed to keep track of time and didn't leave the office until it was pitch dark. I'd spent the afternoon catching up on reports that had been left on my desk, as well as fiddling with a few products our development department wanted me to check out, that I completely missed any further opportunities to talk to Bella. So now I'm on my way home from work with her answer still lingering on my mind.

She's reconsidered. Now what?

That question is answered for me as soon as I enter the penthouse. My home is usually silent when I get home, aside from the bustling of Mrs. Rosemary when she's cleaning or cooking. Tonight, however, I hear chatter in the kitchen. With a cautious gait, I walk toward the voices and come around the corner to see Bella talking to Mrs. Rosemary. They both notice my entrance into the room and stop talking mid-sentence to look at me.

"Bella?" I say.

"I know it's a bit presumptuous to just show up, but I took the chance," she explains as Mrs. Rosemary silently leaves the room to give us privacy.

"You're a welcome surprise." I approach her with my hands in my pockets, my posture casual.

"You were buried in work when I left. I poked my head in, and could tell you were in the zone, so I decided not to interrupt you. I came here so we could get a chance to talk properly Besides, I felt it was best not to have our personal conversation at work. You know, since we want to keep those two separate and all."

"I'm glad you're here." I step forward and stand before her. Being so close to her again has me imaging all the things we could do. My voice dips and turns gravelly when I tell her, "I would like that, very much."

Her eyes flare with lust and she licks her lips.

"As I said this morning, I've reconsidered. I've reconsidered this... you and me."

"Hmmm," I smile.

"It's clear that we have a... an attraction to one another."

"Correct." I run my tongue along my bottom lip.

"But the problem is, at the office, you're my superior and I'm your subordinate. Work conflicts and all."

"I wouldn't want you to feel that your job is in jeopardy, I wouldn't allow that to happen to either one of us. I value you. And I want to value you in all ways."

"See, that. What does it mean? You're my boss, but if we were to be, you know, *intimate*, would you still be my boss?"

"Business and pleasure are two separate things for me. It would mean that at work, I'm still your boss. But when we are not at work, we're equals."

She backs into the counter behind her and my arms cage her in.

"Equals," she repeats

"Equals," I confirm.

"And what we do outside of work?"

"Will cause absolutely no interference in what we do *at* work."

"Okay."

"Okay?" I ask, making sure to get full clarification before proceeding. Giving her the last option to back out, not that I want her to by any means.

"It means yes."

"I can't tell you how much I was hoping to hear you say that," I growl as a I lean into her. I run my nose up the slope of her neck, and she tilts her head to make it easier for me. Once I get to her ear, I pull her earlobe into my mouth and tug with my teeth.

"Rules, Ben. We need rules," she breathes.

"After. I need you first. I've been thinking about tasting you for so long. I just need to taste you.

Her breathing is shaky as I pepper kisses along her jaw until I reach her mouth. I tentatively kiss her juicy lips, trying to take my time and relish this kiss. Unfortunately, the animal in me has shown his claws, and with my next kiss, my body presses against hers and my tongue dives into her mouth seeking hers.

I growl in satisfaction as our tongues clash together in animalistic pleasure. Her arms drape around my shoulders, wrapping together at my neck, as I lift her and place her on top of the counter. Now she's at the perfect height for me to fuck her right here and now. As her lips move over mine, nipping at my lower lip, I consider doing just that.

The sound of a chime interrupts the kiss and has me pulling back from her with an annoyed groan and waiting for the voice to begin.

Angus, my electronic home system, recites its scripted alert. "Sir? You have a visitor requesting your presence in the foyer."

I meet Bella's eyes and find curiosity and concern there. I inhale and try to compose myself before speaking to the overhead voice.

"Angus, is this a life or death matter? Or can this be taken care of with a phone call," I speak into the room.

"Sir, you have a business associate waiting for you. A Mr. Su'Dial. His visit is unexpected. He is here with contracts that need your attention."

Bella seems impressed. "That's oddly specific of Alexa to have those details."

"Ma'am, my name is Angus. I am a superior model of technology far more expansive than Alexa. I was built none other than by Mr. Benjamin Adams, himself," the overhead voice responds immediately.

She feigns embarrassment and stifles a laugh.

"Angus is my house system. I developed it last year. Angus is very touchy about being mistaken for Alexa," I explain to Bella. "Thank you, Angus. Please inform Mr. Su'Dial that I will be with him momentarily. Please chime for Mrs. Rosemary to lead him into the library and offer him a drink while he waits," I instruct.

"Very well, sir," Angus says, followed by the end chime, which echoes through the kitchen.

"Very impressive." She smiles. "I should get going. I just wanted to – I don't know – see you and talk about my decision before I lost my nerve."

"You don't have to leave yet. This business will be quick. Then we can talk about us and what this is."

"I really should get home. I've got a tyrant for a boss."

"Stay, Bella. We have so much to talk about," I request, my hand on her knee.

SIGNING CONTRACTS TOOK LONGER THAN I WANTED IT TO. I was anxious to get back to Bella and to continue what we started in the kitchen. We have so much to discuss about our arrangement or whatever this would become between us. I am confident we can keep our private lives separate from work, but I know she is still fearful that our private entanglement may endanger her job. I need to reassure her that regardless of the nature of our relationship, nothing that happens outside of the workplace will harm her position with the company or my view of her as a respected employee.

I'm a closed-off man and nothing from my personal life seeps into the workplace. If that were the case, my entire history would be widely known at Adams Enterprises. My past is in the past, since the tragedies that have in my life, I became disconnected and therefore my life is a mystery to everyone. Little has spilled into the media as I paid a hefty amount to have some of the information changed from actual events. I refuse to have anything that occurs between Bella and myself to not become headline news as well.

After I escort Mr. Su'Dial out of the penthouse, I go looking for Bella. I find her on the couch in the sitting room with her shoes off and her feet tucked under her. She's reading a magazine that has adorned the coffee table for months. I take a seat beside her and smile. My hand goes to her knee and my other arm drapes over the couch behind her head.

"I'm sorry. That took longer than I was hoping. He asked questions that I had already answered for him. Then he started talking sports. I'm sorry to make you wait."

"It's okay. I know how you are when it comes to you and business." She returns my smile with her reply.

"Now, to a topic I would rather concentrate on."

"Oh yeah? What's that?" She puts down the magazine and turns her body towards me before giving me an impish smile.

"The topic of you and me."

As we discuss what we each want out of a potential relationship, I do my best to reassure her regarding her concerns about our ongoing status as boss and employee.

Something about having her beside me in my space relaxes me. She makes me feel like I don't need to be on edge and in charge at all times. I can't explain what it is about her that calms me, but it makes me feel human again, rather than the way I usually feel, which is more like a machine, programmed to have everything organized at all times, to have all the facts nailed down, and to be prepared for every scenario. I don't feel the pressure to have laid out and planned.

I want to press against her again, but I don't want her to think I've got a one-track mind. While it is frequently true, right now I need to pay attention to her cues. She looks exhausted and I note the late hour on my watch.

"You have two choices right now, Bella. You can either stay the night here and I'll have a car drive you home before work, or I can call a car right now to take you home. She looks at me while she contemplates her response, as if she's trying to figure out my motives.

"I think it would be best if I went home tonight."

I nod and pull out my phone. I call my driver and give him instructions, then place the phone on the table.

"The car will be ready in a few minutes."

"Do you have a driver at your disposal at all times?" she asks.

"My driver lives in the building."

"Shit. You didn't wake him up or anything, did you?" she asks with concern.

"This is his job," I say simply.

"How many other women has he driven home so late at night?"

I open my mouth and her hand flies up. "Wait, no. That's none of my business."

"You would be the first," I say to reassure her. A smile forms on her face, then contorts into confusion.

"Right," she says.

"I'm being honest. I haven't. Truthfully, you're the first woman, aside from my household staff, who has been in my home in years."

"Why is that?"

"Stay the night and I'll tell you," I tease.

"Nice try. You don't always get what you want, Ben," she replies playfully.

"Can't blame me for trying."

SEVERAL DAYS SPEED BY BEFORE BELLA AND I HAVE A chance to be alone together outside of the office. We've shared looks here and there, but with her knowing my schedule - we haven't yet touched the new part of our relationship, our personal relationship outside of work.

I plan to change all that this weekend, which begins in two hours. I had flowers delivered to her desk around lunchtime with a note asking her to pack a weekend bag and be ready for the car to pick her up at seven tonight. She hasn't responded to or denied my request. She didn't even act differently when we sat in a meeting together shortly after the flower delivery, but she did say thank you to me quietly as she passed by on the way to her chair across from me.

The fragrance of those flowers traveled throughout the office and attracted attention from each passersby, several of whom stopped by Bella's office to ask her about the lovely blooms and chat with her. I hope she isn't bothered by the attention.

As I am packing up my satchel for the day, my cell chimes with a text. I swipe the screen and see that Henry texted. We chatted for five minutes at the gala about nothing in particular and made tentative plans to get together. This must be his ask.

Henry: Bocce ball this weekend?

Who the hell still plays bocce ball? I think to myself as I roll my eyes.

Me: Have wknd plans. Raincheck?
H: Anyone I know?
Me: MYOB
H: Srsly?
Me: Yes! NOYB.
H: This whole town is my biz. Including you.
Me: Not this time. Call me next week.

I exit my office, and Bella sits up straight as she sees me approaching her office.

"'Til six," I say, rapping my knuckles on the doorway.

She nods and I see her stifle a smile before I turn and walk to the elevator. I can feel her eyes on me and I confirm it when I turn around once I'm standing in the elevator. Our eyes lock on one another until the doors close and the lift is taking me down to ground level.

My phone chimes again. I pull it out of my pocket, ready to give Henry the middle finger emoji, when I see Bella's name on the screen.

Bella: 'Til six

I don't reply to her; I don't want to appear too eager. Instead, I walk out of the building to the car waiting for me at the curb. I hand my bag to Wayne, my driver and get into the back. It's not long before the door opens and I'm in the underground parking in front of the elevator. I note the time on my watch and turn to Wayne standing stoically as he holds my door for me.

"Thank you Wayne, tonight, I need you to pick up Isabella Dubois. She will need to be picked up by seven, her address is the same that you dropped her off to last week. She will have a bag with her. Please make sure the bag is brought up to the penthouse when you bring her back here."

"Yes, sir," he replies, his face showing no emotion.

"Then, for the remainder of the weekend, you are off duty. I won't need your services until Sunday evening. I don't plan to leave the building and all the food should be already prepped."

"Sir." He nods as I walk away.

Angus greets me once I enter my home. He rattles off statistics of stocks for the day until I enter the kitchen. Mrs. Rosemary is at the stove stirring something in a pot and turns to me as I open the fridge.

"Hello, dear. You're home early," she observes.

"Isabella will be joining me this weekend. If you can see that dinner tonight has enough for two, along with any other meals you've prepared for me this weekend. I apologize for the late notice." My voice is suddenly tight. I'm not comfortable with the way her eyes light up as I started talking.

"The whole weekend, sir?" she asks.

"Correct. And after you finish for tonight, Wayne can drive you home, if you like. We do not wish to be bothered for the weekend," I say.

Her eyes light up again.

"Sir, I'm happy to hear this. Very well, will eggplant parmesan be satisfactory for you this evening? I have the sauce almost finished, and I can make sure everything is ready for timing for when you would like to eat dinner. The seasonal vegetables and the pasta should be ready for you when you wish."

"That's perfect. Thank you."

Her smile is filled with happiness as I leave the room. She begins humming softly and I turn.

I recognize that song.

It's a melody from my childhood that my mother used to sing me to sleep at night. Strange that with the recent thoughts of my parents passing, I hear her humming that melody. It strikes me at that moment that Mrs. Rosemary has worked with my family in one manner or another for as long as I can remember. It's been some time since I've had a sentimental thought for my parents. The ice around my heart truly is thawing.

THE ELEVATOR OPENS UP AND BELLA ENTERS MY HOME. I hear the clicking of her high heels as she walks slowly through my space. Mrs. Rosemary greets her and takes her jacket as I appear in the hallway.

Bella is dressed casual, yet classy. She wears a black flared skirt that goes to just above her knees with black flats. Her blouse is black with white polka dots. It's fitted across her chest and loose underneath. Her hair is in a ponytail and her face glows as she smiles at me.

Mrs. Rosemary nods to me and smiles at Bella, then excuses herself. Bella tentatively steps forward and we stand awkwardly in front of another.

"I don't know how to do any of this," she confesses, her hands nervously wringing as she comes to stand before me.

"There's nothing to be worried about. This, what we're doing, is a relationship, even if it is a bit unconventional. We all have different roles, multiple roles we play in various parts of our lives. If you feel better by compartmentalizing those roles, then we will. If you wish to intertwine them, that is fine too. I completely understand that you do not wish to mix the two."

"Wouldn't you rather be in a relationship you can openly discuss at Adams Enterprises?" she asks.

"My private life is mine, always has been. You are a part of that now, though, so it's ours. I own the company, so I can choose what I do and do not disclose. Besides, in the time that you've known me, have you be aware of any of my personal business to be common knowledge? Do you hear gossip about me around the water cooler?"

"I heard you have a monthly dinner date. Aside from that, people say you work too much and go to the gym a lot," she recounts.

"Then I hope you believe me when I say I can keep the relationship separate from work. Although, I will admit, keeping my hands to myself when I see you may be harder on me," I admit.

"How so?" she asks.

"I'm only a man and my thoughts aren't always of the purest nature when it comes to you, especially when I imagine you on my desk, or against the windows of my office. "

"Only a man, eh?" She laughs at my choice of words.

"I don't know what it is about you." I reach out and clasp both of her hands in mine as I look up to the ceiling. "You get me to say things that I wouldn't."

"I am, after all, one of a kind." She laughs.

"Dinner will be ready in a moment. I hope you like eggplant. Once I learn your tastes, I can better accommodate your preferences."

"Ben. It's okay. You don't have to reorganize everything for me or cater to me. Whatever you want to eat is fine. As long as it's edible, I'm usually game for anything. I grew up on a farm, so it's not like I'm picky," she says, placing her hand on the collar of my shirt.

The elevator opens again, this time with Wayne bringing in Bella's bag. I catch his eye and ask him to drive Mrs. Rosemary home so Bella and I can be alone.

I set Angus to sleep mode so there will be no interruptions from him, so Bella and I can finally be alone.

For the whole weekend.

Together.

And hopefully naked.

CHAPTER SEVEN

BENJAMIN

IT'S NOT A NORMAL OCCURRENCE THAT I EAT A PRIVATE meal with this beautiful woman. I've shared meals in the presence of Bella, with other associates and with friends once upon a time - but tonight dinner has a whole new meaning.

Tonight is the beginning of something I can't quite name.

Tonight is the beginning of something I can't wait to start.

Bella seems slightly nervous, and honestly a small part of myself is as well. With the sweeping of her hair behind her ear, the glances she steals when she thinks I'm not paying attention along with the fidgeting of her hands she can't stay still. It's cute.

Dinner is delicious. After we finish, and I clear our plates, she smiles hesitantly at me.

"Ben," she starts as she stands and turns in my direction. "All weekend? Why?" she asks.

"Because I don't want us leaving our castle. I want to focus completely on you and I don't want to share you with anyone. I want to get to know a different you and what better way than closing us up in here alone together all weekend."

"Talk about moving fast." She laughs nervously.

"I'm not expecting anything. We don't have to do anything you don't want to do. If we end up talking all weekend, then so be it. We'll get to know one another that much better. But we end up naked all weekend." I shrug. "Then that's even better."

"Someone is confident." she says with a smile.

"Isabella," I say, walking up to her. I catch her eyes by leaning down and placing my hands on her arms. "I'm a sure thing." I wink and lean in to kiss her forehead.

As I begin to pull away, her hand catches mine and she holds firm, not allowing me to move away. Her eyes dark and fierce, she purrs, "So am I."

Our bodies react first as my body gravitates to hers. I pull her face to mine just as a shaky breath is released from her lips and press my lips to hers. Her hands find purchase in the front of my shirt before releasing the fabric and moving her hands around to my back. My hands move from cradling her head, down to her lower back, putting pressure there and pulling her into me.

My cock has its own heartbeat. It demands to be released from my pants and closer to her.

She moans lightly into my mouth as I break away. My hand fumbles for the zipper on her skirt, once my fingers find the clasp, I begin to pull it down. I pull my mouth away from her for a slight moment.

"Is this okay?" I gruffly ask her.

"Yes." She hisses and pulls me back to her. I unzip her skirt and it pools at her feet. I then grab the back of her upper thighs to pick her up as her legs wrap around my waist. I carry her through my home towards my bedroom.

It's been years since I've been with anyone. I've kept myself busy over the years to be celibate and not act on my carnal desires. That worked until Bella came into my life and now I can't bring myself to slow down. I don't want to, she is everything and I want to be close to her in every way possible.

I want her.

I must have her.

She kisses up my neck to my ear and tugs on it with her teeth as I gently lay her down on the soft surface of my bed.

"Wait." She stops us. "I need to say this, so we're completely up front and honest with each other, since we're doing this."

I pull back and wait for her to continue.

"I'm clean. Like, squeaky clean. I'm no virgin, but it's been... well, it's been a long time. But we don't need to get into the details right now."

"Straight to the point." I smile.

"I just want to be open and honest. I thought you should know."

"In that case, I'll let you know I haven't fucked anyone in ten or so years."

I lean in, prepared to take her mouth with mine, but am denied when her hand goes to my chest and pushes me away.

""Okay, hold up," she insists.

"We don't need to go into the specifics right now," I say, repeating her words back to her.

"Fair enough, but will you?"

I look at her and I nod. "I promise that I will."

What is it with this woman? She makes me feel like a different person. She gets me to talk, to question, to do things I normally wouldn't. It's not just because I have her here in my bedroom, it's because she makes me want to open up. I have the need to open up to her.

To build the need back up, we make out, which is something I haven't done in years, too many to count. I determine that I like kissing. Correction: I love kissing her. Our tongues dance together to an unknown beat as we each get to know the way the other kisses. Our hands explore every inch of the other's body within reach.

My fingers itch to feel all of her, her skin, her softness, her wetness.

"Ben," she moans as my mouth moves to her neck and trails kisses down to her collarbone, leaving goose bumps in my wake. She cranes her head back so I can get more of her. As she arches her back, my hand finds her breast. I squeeze as I lift it up, while my head bends down to meet the swell of her breast. I kiss the cleavage my hand creates and begin to pull down the lace of her bra covering her. She helps me move her blouse aside, while also pushing into my touch more. Her hand reaches out as my mouth makes contact with her sensitive flesh and she holds my head to her as I suck on her tits with fever. I circle and lick around her nipple, pull the peak into my mouth, rolling it against my tongue and lightly nipping it with my teeth. I add light suction when she arches her body into me and moans lightly in pleasure. My other hand squeezes her other breast, then I shift my mouth to it to keep her body purring for me as I pull down the cup of her bra.

She sighs loudly and grabs for me to come up from my assault on her chest. When my mouth and hers collide again, she murmurs against my lips.

"Clothes," she directs.

As if that were the magic word to get naked together, my cock manages to become even harder than it was, which is a feat since my cock is pure stone already. Her fingers are on the buttons of my shirt, pulling each button through swiftly. I clutch the bottom of her shirt and lift. She pulls her arms up and her shirt is off and on the floor. I take a moment to back off slightly to take in her beauty. I smile as her fingertips tease along the top of her bra. Her black lace bra is beautiful, but I've determined that it is in my way. I want to see her, all of her.

It's like she reads my mind as her fingers flick the front clasp and frees her breasts from their prison.

My eyes zero in on the movement of her breasts bouncing from the confines of her bra. I run my tongue along my upper lip, brushing against my teeth in anticipation.

Her nipples are perfect.

Her body is amazing.

My eyes trail the length of her exposed ivory skin and my mouth salivates for her.

I want her.

I come to stand in front of her, admiring the view of her laying in my bed.

I look down at her now and note her matching black lace panties. I bend in closer to her, lay one knee on the bed and smile. My fingertip drags over the edge of her panties and down the middle of the damp fabric that barely covers her pussy.

A low moan escapes her parted lips as I dip my hand into her panties and come into contact with the moisture gathering between her legs. I dip my fingers into her and her channel is so fucking tight. My fingers are being squeezed like vise. She moans softly and arches her back, allowing my fingers to go deeper into her. I pull my fingers in and out, switching between having my fingers inside her to strumming her clit like I'm playing a guitar, playing the chords with ease as I bring her to orgasm quickly by lightly massaging her button. My fingers move in and out with the ease from the wetness of her orgasm. Her breathing is quick and her heartbeat is rapid as I withdraw my fingers. I make sure that her eyes are on me as I lick her juices off of my fingers with a satisfied smile.

"Mouth-watering." I murmur.

I remove my shirt and her gaze lingers over my chest. Her eyes follow as I reach down to unbuckle my belt and undo the button of my jeans slowly. Her eyes move across my skin with no shame, then I see her tremble as she lets out a breath as if she'd been holding it since I made her come.

"I could say the same about you," she says shyly.

"You have yet to taste me, but you will," I say, my voice gravelly.

I reach my hand inside my boxer briefs and rub the same fingers that were just inside her, against my swollen cock, then grab the waistband and tug those down as well.

My cock springs out and stands to attention. Bella's gaze lands on it as she licks her lips. Her attention is held captive.

"Come here," she beckons boldly.

As I stand before her, her eyes are still on my cock. She grabs me by the hips, then looks up at me as if asking permission to put her mouth on me. When I nod, she grabs my cock and swallows me down.

"Fuck!" I exclaim. I did not expect her to be so bold.

After a minute with her mouth on my cock, the need to be inside her is strong and I pull her off. I push her up on the bed and cover her body with mine.

My lips take hers and I plunge my tongue into her mouth. My cock is planted right between her legs and nudging at her entrance. She gasps at the contact, and I smile as I press into her. At the same time, she moves her hips in time with mine, then parts her legs wider and moans into my mouth as I gently thrust. When I am fully seated in her warm pussy, I sigh and lean up on my elbows.

"I want to fuck you," I say. "I need to fuck you."

"Isn't that what we are doing?" she breathes.

"I mean, I don't want to be gentle," I grind out, my hips still gently thrusting. Her hips rise to adjust the angle.

"Then don't," she says. Her mischievous smile immediately transforms into a look of surprise as I rear back and then slam into her.

I power my thrusts, fucking her like I've imagined doing since the moment our eyes met in my office that first day.

The room fills with the sounds of our bodies moving against one another, the gasps out of both of our mouths, as our pleasure builds. My hand goes to her hip as I thrust; her hand on my shoulder pulls me closer to her. Our teeth clash as I kiss her with as much passion as I can. I will never get enough of kissing her.

Once the kissing becomes so frenzied as to be nearly combative, I lean back to look in her eyes. We fuck with our gazes locked. She spreads her legs wider for me and wraps them around my middle, pushing me in with her heels.

I lean down and roughly take her lips again. With my cock spreading her open, pushing in and out, my body wants nothing more than to release. But she needs to go first, as hard it is for me to hold off.

"Oh god!" she cries out. "I'm... I'm..." It's as if she read my mind.

"Come, baby. Come on my cock."

She lets out a satisfied groan and her pussy squeezes my cock, which prompts my own climax to begin. We moan in pleasure together, both of our bodies tight with release. I languidly thrust my hips as I milk the remainder of my orgasm. Her pussy, still tight and squeezing me, feels absolutely amazing.

I lean my forehead to her shoulder and breathe her in. She smells like a mixture of flowers and sweet sweat. I open my eyes and look down at the space between our bodies. Goosebumps cover her body, so I lean up and grab the blanket that is bunched at our feet to cover her. I gingerly climb out of bed to grab a washcloth from the adjoining bathroom. Once I've tenderly cleaned her and wiped myself off as well, I toss the rag towards the bathroom's tile floor. As I lay on my back, Bella clutches the covers tightly around her breasts and sighs. I turn my head towards her and observe her profile until she turns her head towards me.

"That was... That was...some good sex." She says with a lazy smile as she relaxes into the pillows.

She looks content, exhausted, but content to stay where she is.

I like the way she looks in my bed.

CHAPTER EIGHT

BELLA

I DIDN'T EXPECT IT TO BE THAT GOOD. I DIDN'T EXPECT JUST one night could have me falling for him. I'm not supposed to fall for him. It's not allowed; we work together. Our relationship will need to remain a secret. But can I do that?

I see the way he is with others: he's a crass jerk. But with me, he's the opposite. He's different with me than how I've seen him with other people, more relaxed. I'm not entirely sure why, but I'm willing to stick around find out. I know I can't change him overnight, but perhaps I can help others see he isn't the monster he's worked so hard to portray over the years.

He's not a beast; he's a prince.

The sunlight in creeping in from the haphazardly closed curtains in his bedroom. I'm not entirely sure how early it is, but my body feels rested and a little sore from last night. Ben clears his throat and wraps his arms around me, then pulls me into his body. When his nose brushes against my hair and he breathes me in, it pulls me out of my thoughts.

"What's going on in that mind of yours?" he mumbles.

"Nothing. I'm just reveling in the moment," I reply, turning my face toward his. Our lips are inches apart and Ben closes the distance to lightly brush our lips together.

"I don't believe that for a second. You're the most vocal woman I know. I think that you always speak what is on your mind. I'd guess you're thinking about something related to what's happening here tonight. Am I right?" His attempt to draw me out is endearing, but I'm not ready to talk about it yet.

"I'm thinking about how good you are at this."

"This?" he asks, flexing his hips against me, his cock hardening again.

"I want you again," I whisper against his lips. "I don't want to talk anymore."

Ben rolls me to my stomach, his hands trace my back from the top of my shoulder and following my spine. His hands clutch onto the globes of my ass, massaging me and then I feel his finger breaching my entrance. His hips surge forward, his cock solid at my entrance and parting my pussy as he continues to push inside. I suck in a breath and hold it until he's spread me completely. He feels so good, filling me up and possessing me. Our moans echo through the room as his thrusts turn wild, unhinged, and he bucks out of control against me. Then he slows down his movements and languidly pushes in and out of me. My back arching as my entire body feels amazing. I'm trembling, tense with the arousal he's building in me as he pumps his hips over and over. I slide my hand down my front and the tip of my point finger and middle finger finds my clit and I start rubbing the nub. I'm already half-way there when suddenly one more swipe of my fingers and I have the need to scream his name as I come harder than I did last night. My vision goes white and a silent scream tears from my mouth as he continues to drive his cock in and out of me, building me up to another orgasm immediately and pressing against my core each time he sinks into me.

My heart thunders inside my chest and the room spins as we come together again. His loud groan drowns out my breathy gasps. He slows his movements, while my pussy milks his cock as the last tremors of my orgasm ripple through my body.

We're silent as Ben pulls out of me, leaving my body feeling boneless and empty. He falls back against the bed and throws his arm over his eyes as he takes a satisfied breath. I turn to look at him and see him smiling, I can't help but smile as well as I rotate my body toward him and snuggle into his side. His places an arm around me and rolls me closer to him, holding me against his body.

"Fuck. I didn't know it would be this good," he says, mirroring my exact thought from moments ago.

I'M NOT SURE HOW LONG WE LIE IN BED TOGETHER, caressing each other, stealing kisses here and there, telling each other our secrets. By the time we rise out of the warmth of his bed, it is dark out, and we have wasted the entire day. We order in dinner, then sit on the couch, a spread of Chinese food in front of us, and eat out of the takeover cartons. As I shovel chow mein into my mouth like I haven't eaten in days, Ben uses his chopsticks to grab a piece of beef from the carton in my hand. We eat in companionable silence and smile while we chew.

This is not at all how I expected the weekend to go. Sure, I assumed we would have sex. But I didn't think we would be so normal, like any other couple.

Are we a couple? We agreed to have a relationship outside of the office, but would that mean that I'm his girlfriend and he's my boyfriend? This is new territory for me in the realm of who we are, so I'm not sure how to approach it.

Off in the distance a phone chimes, and, for a split second, I see Ben pause his chewing. I expect him to get up and check his phone, but he surprises me by staying beside me and continuing to eat.

This isn't the Benjamin Adams that I know. This is someone else.

After a few moments, I notice that he's still ignoring his phone and it's definitely different than how he is at work. It doesn't bother me, but I don't want him to feel like he needs to ignore the outside world when we're together. Time and life doesn't stop when we are here in his penthouse together.

"Are you going to go and check that?" I ask.

"I wasn't planning to. This is a no-work weekend," he declares as he reaches into my carton with his chopsticks again.

"Do you have no-work weekends regularly? I mean, sometimes I have emails from you at all hours of the night, every day of the week."

"I'm trying something different," he offers.

"Something different," I repeat.

He puts down his chopsticks and the carton he's holding and turns to me, his knee bending and his arm going over the back of the couch behind me.

"When we are together, I don't want to have any distractions. Will that be how it always is?" He pauses then shrugs. "I doubt it, but we just started this. I want to give you all of me."

I smile at his choice of words. *All of him. The good, the bad and the... charming.*

"My view of you, it's very professional, very work-focused. So, it may take me some time to get used to you putting work on hold, especially since I pressure you at work for certain things. But I like the thought of getting all of you."

"Will you give me all of you?" he asks nervously. *Nervous. Benjamin Adams is nervous about my answer!*

"I'll give you everything," I reply in honesty.

I want to give him all of me.

I want him.

CHAPTER NINE

BENJAMIN

I'T'S SUNDAY NIGHT AND I STILL HAVEN'T GOTTEN MY FILL of Bella. We've spent a healthy amount of time talking, making love and getting used to one another. Now that I've had her, I want more of her. With her, it's as if I'm under a spell. She gets me to talk, she gets me to look at things from a different angle, and best of all, she makes me feel.

I haven't felt this depth of emotion in years. Frankly, I wasn't expecting it to ever come back. But here she is, draped in a sheet as she studies the collections in my library. Seeing her here, in my space, makes me feel things I didn't know were still in me. Her fingertips touch every book, and her face reflects a sense of awe, while her lips try on the titles as she goes. She looks up and down the shelves and finally comes to stand in the middle of the room, drops the sheet, opens her arms, and twirls with her head back.

I stand in the doorway, leaning my shoulder against the wooden door frame, my sweats hanging low on my hips. With my arms cross over my chest, I observe her.

I've never seen anyone look at my space with such wonder

until now. As I watch her expression of pure joy, I realize what a privilege it is to see it through her eyes. I'm not sure I've ever looked at this room the way she is. I've come to take my home and possessions for granted, but having her here lets me see it through fresh eyes, and I can easily see how amazing this room can be.

When she completes her final turn, she looks at me over her shoulder and smiles.

"How come I didn't know you are a bibliophile?" she asks, turning on her heel, then bending to pick up the discarded sheet. She drapes it around her again and saunters toward me. I stand straight, centered in the doorway, as she approaches.

I watch her, observing the way the light from the fireplace is hitting her features, and the smattering of freckles on her shoulders as she moves about the library. The lust in her eyes and the mischievous upturn of her lips all strike me like a physical blow, making my chest tighten and my head spin. When she stands in front of me, all I can think about is having her again.

She tilts her head and studies me. Part of me would give every book in this library to know what she sees when she looks at me that way. Before I can voice the offer, she places her hands on my hips and pulls our bodies together. My cock stands to attention again and she acknowledges it with a coy smile.

"I like this dressed down version of you," she says quietly as she stands on her tip-toes and leans into me, her lips brushing against my jaw. I smile as I wrap my arms around her waist and hoist her up against my body.

"I quite like this naked version of you." I lean in and nip at her bottom lip before pressing my lips against hers. "Very, very, very much."

I press her against the wall outside my library and take her mouth with mine. I grind myself against her and growl in satisfaction. The scent of her arousal tempts me past my limit and

I'm so fucking turned on that I can't help but take her right here. I pull my cock out of my sweatpants and slide into her.

I pump my hips into her quickly, relishing the feeling of her pussy being wrapped around my cock. Her tight channel squeezes me, fitting my cock perfectly, as if she were made for me. My hands clutch the globes of her ass as my knees bend to slide my cock in and out of her warmth at a slightly different angle. Our mingled breaths are heavy as I fuck her against the wall, her legs wrapped around my waist and her nails dragging through the skin on my shoulders.

My loud groan echoes through the house as I press into her, then my hips thrust two more times before I hit my climax. I switch my pace and continue to pump languidly as her pussy grasps my cock when she reaches her orgasm with a happy sigh, pulling me into her, her fingers continuing to dig into my shoulders.

My cock slips out of her, then she unwraps her legs and slides down.

I get down on one knee and watch my come slide down her leg.

"What are you doing?" she asks, lifting her hand on the top of my head and running her fingers through my short hair.

"Just admiring my handiwork," I reply with a satisfied smirk.

CHAPTER TEN

BENJAMIN

"Fuck off!" I say to Elliot, one of my oldest friends and now my newest *former* friend, as he stands in front of my desk.

"I've vetted everything for this plan. I want to help out the folks around the beach areas who have the lack of resources that both yourself and I do. Benjamin, I know deep down inside, you care about the less fortunate." Elliot begs. "We used to be so close, man. Come on, we've known each other for years. I knew you before...before you became the man you are today. Hell, we were going to be business partners. "

"Be that as it may, I don't give two shits about whatever cause you want my name on. I don't trust anything that comes out of your mouth and that's all that I have to say."

"It's not your name I want. I'm offering this to join teams, to work on something together. To reconnect."

"Interesting, since I haven't seen you in all these years, not since the accident. Interesting how now you want to do business together – to fucking reconnect! – when my business is soaring.

How, after so many years of silence, do you think it's perfectly fine to come to me now?" I snarl.

"Listen, she was important to me too." Elliot switches his tactics.

I fight the urge to jump up and pummel him. I don't want to talk about this shit.

"Of course she was; you were fucking her, weren't you? That's probably another reason why you haven't come around once I found out about you two. You were having an affair with my fiancée for, what, a year?" I say cruelly. "The bottom line here is that you are not someone I want to work with and definitely not someone I want to have any connection with in my life."

"Ben. I'm sorry. I was a shit friend." He stops talking when I hold up my hand to silence him. My irritation has been growing with every word that falls out of his mouth.

"Elliot, you aren't my friend, obviously not then and absolutely not now. I will *not* do business with you. You can see yourself out. Immediately. And don't make any more fake appointments with my assistant."

Elliot stands. His gaze burns into me.

"Why can't we let the past be the past?" he demands petulantly.

"Because the past is what created the man I am now."

"So then you should be thanking me." His tone is cocky.

"If you'd like to think you are the reason for my success, be my guest. Just do it somewhere else." I wave him off, desperately wanting this conversation to be over. I don't have time to argue with him. What the fuck is he thinking?

"You just said—"

"I said the past created the man I am now. The past is more than any one single event you might have had some play in. In all reality, my parents dying, being thrust into leadership of this company, my fiancée dying, and then..." I take a deep breath and refocus. "You know what, I don't need to explain myself to you. I would like you to leave." I slam my hand on the desk, done with this interruption to my day once and for all.

I push the button on the phone for Bella. When her sweet voice comes on, I ask her to come into my office. My voice contains venom, which I don't need to be giving her.

She opens the door and freezes in the doorway likely noticing the tension between Elliot and myself. She looks between us, hesitantly she announces herself.

"I would like you to get security on the line to get up here and see Mr. Hunter out of my office. And make sure security knows he isn't to step foot in here again."

"Oh c'mon, Ben." Elliot rolls his eyes and holds up his hand.

"Get. Out," I bellow.

With a huff, Elliot leaves my office, whipping past Bella as she lingers in the doorway.

"Need anything else?" she asks quietly once he's gone.

"You," I say simply.

"You know the rules," she scolds with a smile, her hand resting on the handle of my office door.

"Close the door, Isabella. Lock it," I direct.

She studies me for a moment, then turns her head to look into the office area Having seen nothing to dissuade her, she swiftly does what I asked and then approaches the desk. I hit the button under my desk to close the blinds, push my chair out, and pat my lap. With a small hesitation she sits down and her arm drapes behind my back.

"Ben," she warns. "We promised to keep this separate. You aren't doing a good job of that right now."

"The point is that we have been keeping things separate so far. Not once have we done or said anything inappropriate here. Right now, though, I need to release this tension and if that breaks the rules, then so be it. I need my woman, even if it's just her presence or a simple kiss."

"Can't you just...?" Her words trail off as she looks down to my lap.

I pierce her with a look and she fights off a smile. "I've been jacking off to you nightly for months. I would rather not have to do that anymore."

"How can I take care of you today, Mr. Adams? Something more than just a kiss perhaps? If we're breaking the rules – just this once – we better go big or go home, right?" she says playfully.

I smile, enjoying the fact that she is game to bend the rules and falling just a little bit in love with her in this moment. The thought that I could love her is startling, but I don't push it away.

"There are a few options, but I think right now, I would like you on your knees under my desk while I make a phone call."

She slides off my lap and onto her knees. She reaches my belt and begins to tug.

"Take me out and stroke me," I instruct her, my tone heavy with anticipation.

She smiles eagerly and follows my instructions.

Stroke one. Stroke two. Stroke three. Drops of precum forms on the tip of my cock and she looks to me for guidance.

"Lick it," I instruct.

She nods and leans in. Her tongue flattens and she licks my entire swollen tip with a throaty moan.

"Take me in your mouth and suck me off. Make me come and tonight, I'll take care of you in any way you request."

Bella licks the tip of my cock as she flattens her tongue again prior to taking my shaft into her mouth then pulls up my cock and hollows out her cheeks as she applies light suction. I grab my cell phone off my desk then lean back in my chair. After pulling up a phone number, I click "call" and wait for the line to connect.

"Yes. James Ryder, please?" I breathe out. I regain some composure as I wait to speak with James, and my hand reaches for Bella's shoulder. She pulls and sucks with skill, her hand stroking the shaft where her mouth doesn't reach. She takes me as far as she can go, my cockhead hitting the back of her throat every other beat as the call connects.

I listen as I'm greeted, then say "I was thinking we should work on a project together." I listen to his positive response, then begin speaking again. "I was considering the idea you brought up when we were playing racquetball last year..." He speaks and I listen, but barely, as Bella bobs up and down on me. "Yes, I'm aware that was last year. You know I like to take my time thinking over business matters." I manage to say all the words as if nothing were happening, but follow them with a loud grunt, which is noticed on the other end of my phone. I laugh it off, but Bella's movements quicken. She wiggles her tongue against the underside of my cock and hums.

"Yes, let's get together over dinner next week and work out the details. Maybe we can move things forward in a few months..." My head hits the back of the chair, my voice trailing off.

"Yesssssss," I hiss as I release into her mouth. My come splatters against the back of her throat as she swallows every drop.

Remembering myself, I try to cover my outburst by responding, "Yes. I'll see that Bella makes the arrangement with your assistant..." Bella releases my cock from her mouth, and it flops to my stomach and points up at me. Satisfied. She wipes her mouth and smiles up at me from where she's still seated on the floor between my legs. Her gaze is filled with heated desire and a bit of self-satisfaction.

"Very well. Next week," I reply to James and end the call. I place my cell of the top of my desk and look down at her.

"Better?" she asks.

"You suck my cock like it belongs in your mouth. I feel like the weight of the world has been lifted from my shoulders, that all of everything from earlier has melted away."

CHAPTER ELEVEN

BENJAMIN

I've made it my mission to fuck Bella at the office, and each day for the three months since she sucked my cock under the desk that day, I have tried to make it happen. Thoughts of fucking her on every surface in this building constantly fill my mind. But the woman is stubborn and hasn't given in to my wishes. I understand, though; I'm not a complete asshole. Besides, the game is fun.

Over that same period of time, we've worked during the day and fucked during the night. She's stayed at my condo more often than her own and I find that I rather enjoy having her in my space.

Today, we're sitting in a meeting discussing a potential joint venture with James Ryder's company, Ryder Tech. Halfway through the meeting, it becomes clear to me that I have pissed off Bella with something I've said. She is staring daggers at me. When my eyes meet hers, I flick my palms up and mouth *what?* She rolls her eyes and scribbles furiously on her notepad. While I expect her to hand over a note to me, she just continues scribbling and leans her head toward the side of the table where my purchasing director is sitting. He's talking about what components would be needed on our company's end to launch the venture.

I watch her as she nods her head and continues to ignore me. When I have something to add to the conversation, her eyes stay on her notes and never meet mine. I look around the table as I speak and notice all eyes are on me, except for hers.

At the end of the meeting, I stand, button my jacket, and step aside to shake hands with everyone as Bella brushes past me, looking furious.

Before I can get out of the conference room, Maggie stops me. By asking to have a word with me, she has unknowingly stopped me from going after my girlfriend. I'm slightly pissed off about it, since I want to confront whatever situation is occurring with Bella, but in this time and place, I need to put work first.

"With this joint venture, Ben, we may have some hourly staff working overtime. We haven't budgeted for overtime in those specific departments."

"How many salaried employees do we have on staff?" I ask.

"Not enough." She shakes her head.

I groan and run my palm roughly over my face as I bend my neck back. I didn't put much thought into that, and now I'm regretting advancing on the plans so quickly. I try to think of a solution, then look at Maggie.

"Within the project scope, we will need to set clear limits regarding which team members can and cannot work the overtime. I do not want full teams to work overtime."

"But that puts more work on some staff and not as much as on others." She has a point, but I brush it off.

"Those folks will be rewarded with overtime pay. Isn't that enough?" The bite in my bark is not intended really for Maggie. I just want out of this conversation.

"Ben, can you give me an org chart of the teams you will be

creating? Perhaps those individuals are salaried employees and if you want anyone specific added, we can change their exemption status."

"How come there are hourly and salaried employees? Wouldn't it be more logical to have one or the other?" I question.

"Your father wanted a mixture. There are positions within Adams Enterprises that do not need to be salaried. And some that clearly do."

"Can we set a time to meet and discuss each staff member's status? I would like to see where we can make these sort of changes within the company. Salaried employees allow for more work to be done, due to their longer hours and static pay."

"While you may have staff here who prefer to be hourly so they can reap that overtime." Maggie nods.

"You know everyone here better than I do. Perhaps we meet next week?" I suggest.

"Something is different about you," she observes, crossing her arms and eyeing me.

"Pardon?" I tilt my head.

"You're asking, rather than demanding. You're willing to discuss rather than blindly change. What's happening here?" Maggie steps back, hands on her hips, and looks me up and down as if she will find the magic answer to my recent change in demeanor.

"Nothing's different, Maggie. It's your imagination." I laugh and brush her off as we exit the room.

"No. Something is definitely different about you." She follows behind me as she struggles to keep up with my long strides.

I've made it to the door of my office. I want to be left alone and yet I need to speak with Bella. I can't very well do that with the mother hen of HR standing next to me.

"Maggie, I beg you, let it be. I'm the same man I've been since forever. Rest assured, my body has not been taken over by an alien or a parasite." I force a laugh.

"No, you are less angry. More simpatico."

"Maggie," I say, my tone contains a warning.

She holds both her hands up in surrender. "Fine. Fine. You big brute. You're still the scary, mean CEO... Oh, I'm so scared!" she jokes as she walks away.

I shake my head and look around the space. I peek into Bella's office and see her with her head buried in the screen of her computer. I go into her office and quietly shut the door behind me. The click of the door brings her head up and we lock eyes.

"Ben. Not now," she says, her voice stern.

"What happened? Why are you pissed? What did I do?" I ask her in rapid succession.

"Oh, *you* can see that I'm pissed? Good of you to be so fucking observant. Congratu-fucking-lations, Ben!" she bites.

"I have no idea what is going on, so please help me understand?" I say as calmly as I can. I'm unprepared for a fight and I'm not exactly sure what I'm dealing with here. It's been a while since I've dealt with someone else's feelings.

"Understand? Ben, you're pulling me out as your assistant and offering me up to that other company as if I'm expendable. It's like a slap across the face. That's what you're doing."

I try to think back to the meeting and where she got that information and I'm coming up empty. She looks at me and stands. She grabs her cell phone and starts throwing random things from her desk drawers into her purse with finality. I walk around her desk and grab her wrist to halt her.

"Stop it. What are you doing?" I seethe through my teeth.

"I'm leaving," she rages right back to me. She turns to face me. We are inches apart, and all I want to do is shut her up by kissing her.

"You can't just leave," I say, biting back a laugh at my first thoughts and stepping away from her.

"My employment here is at-will. I'm under no contract to work for you, so I can quit anytime. And that, sir, is what I am doing – effective now!" She points to the ground for emphasis.

"Isabella!" I say with so much anger. "There is no chance in hell I would send you to work anywhere that I'm not. I don't want you to work anywhere else. I don't want you anywhere but by my side. What I was implying in that meeting – and maybe it wasn't conveyed correctly – was that you would work closely with their CEO's assistant and maybe some of their staff. But you would not be leaving this company."

"That's not what I heard in there," she retorts, crossing her arms stubbornly.

"Hey, you heard wrong. If I have any control over you, it's that. You are still working here and if you ever leave me, there better be a fucking good reason." My anger and frustration boils. She looks at me, really looks at me with steady eyes.

"Wait. If I quit here... did you think that also means I quit you?" she asks, her tone changing to worry.

"Wouldn't that be what you would do?" I ask, almost fearing of her answer.

"No, Ben. I mean, it would likely make our relationship easier because we wouldn't have to hide, but if I stopped working for you, I wouldn't stop being *with* you."

"No?" I ask.

"Not a chance. I kind of like you. You're my beast – at work and in the sack." She smiles as she whispers the last part.

"I wasn't trying to make you feel like you were expendable. You are far from it." I pull her to me and wrap my arms around her. She head lays against my chest and wraps her arms around my middle in return. I kiss the top of her head and move one my hands so that my hand holds her head to me.

"If I'm your Beast, you're my Beauty," I say quietly.

"Ugh. I did what I never wanted to do."

"What's that?" I ask as she pulls herself out of my arms.

"I brought our relationship into work."

"Does that mean that I can bend you over the desk and fuck you?"

"Benjamin!" She holds my gaze. Her annoyance is tempered with mirth.

"Can't blame a guy for trying." I laugh. "Are we clear though? The conversation in the meeting? I would never... I don't want you leaving here. I just want to make sure you are fully aware of that. You are stuck with me. I'm a better person with you around."

She looks at me with unshed tears in her eyes and nods.

"We're clear. And thank you." She smiles.

"For what?" I ask. *Why is she thanking me?*

"For fighting. For stopping me and explaining what I misunderstood."

"Next time, don't run. I'm not holding you prisoner, but if you were ever to quit, I would at least hope we can talk through it before it reaches that point."

"I promise."

"The same goes for our personal relationship. No running."

"No running," she agrees, leaning into me.

My arms wrap around her and I bend down to take her lips softly with mine. Our connection lasts mere seconds before the office door opens and we jerk apart.

I wipe my face and look to whoever intruded on our moment. I meet the surprised eyes of Maggie. She opens and closes her mouth, unsure what to say. She quickly steps further into the office and shuts the door behind her.

"What the hell did I just walk into?" she whisper-shouts at us, slamming the folder she was holding onto the desk in front of us.

"Nothing," Bella and I say in unison.

"Bullshit. That was definitely *not* nothing."

"Listen, Maggie," I start, but she holds up her hand in a request for silence.

"I need to speak to both of you, but separately. Benjamin, please leave Isabella's office. Do not leave the building; I will be in your office shortly." She points to the door. "Fucking HR nightmare," she mumbles.

Like an obedient child, I follow her directions. I offer a sympathetic look to Bella and mouth that I'm sorry before leaving her office.

I pace my office for what feels like an eternity before Maggie comes in, she closes the door and strides to the chair behind my desk. *My* chair. She points to the guest chair opposite her as she takes a seat.

"Maggie, listen," I say. "We're adults here. And this is my company."

"I've spoken with Isabella and she has confirmed that you did not force yourself on her."

"Damn straight, I didn't. We're together; we have a relationship. It's separate from work."

"Ben, how could it be separate from work? Work is a part of who you are. It's a part of who we all are." Maggie frowns.

"Once work is over, we are different people. We don't talk to one another as boss and assistant. We're equals."

"While I have seen the change with you, and I love the fact that you have opened up to someone else, it's not professional to be in a relationship with your employee, especially an employee who reports directly to you. How can you be objective?"

I don't know how to answer that question. I try to think if I could handle a situation where I needed to be objective and I'm not entirely sure that I could. Have I made a mistake by getting involved with Bella? Was my attraction to her something I should have ignored?

I look Maggie in the eyes. "I appreciate you and what you do here, Maggie. But, as previously discussed, there is nothing in our employee handbooks forbidding fraternization between staff members. I hope that you will not hold anything against Isabella regarding what you walked in on. We will do better not to show any physical affection while at work. That was my mistake and I apologize. And I apologize for putting you in this position."

She shakes her head. "Ben, I wish it were that simple," she says, her tone full of regret.

"It *is* that simple. I'm the owner of this company and there are no grounds to do anything to Isabella's employment status here. I refuse to let you make her an example," I say firmly.

"Adams Enterprises cannot be seen as a company where employees do whatever they want, that's there is no meaning between a boss and their staff? Other staff members may see your relationship as an opportunity, and from that opportunity could come harassment lawsuits."

"This relationship has been going on for almost four months, Maggie. Up until now, have you suspected anything going on between the two of us?" I ask.

"Aside from the photos from the gala, no," she admits hesitantly.

"Then, like I said before, we will continue to refrain from being anything more than boss and employee at work. I do not want work to dictate my life. She's become a part of my life, and I do not want that to change."

Maggie takes a deep breath. "Ben. I'm happy for you. Really, I am. I don't want anything to interfere with your happiness again," she says sadly.

"Then don't take it away from me," I plead.

She looks shocked at my begging. She observes me quietly as I wait for her to speak. I would get on my hands and knees if that would help. I'm split open right now, begging someone who has known me almost all my life to let me continue what could be seen from the outside looking in, a forbidden relationship, but it's a relationship that is so right in so many ways.

CHAPTER TWELVE

BELLA

I STAYED FAR AWAY FROM BEN FOR THE REST OF THE DAY. After Maggie left my office, I was walking on eggshells in fear of losing my job or pissing off someone who may or may not have heard that the CEO of Adams Enterprises and I were found in a compromising position in my office.

Is this my last day of work? Am I going to be fired?

Is this the last day I will have the chance to kiss Ben? Is he going to break up with me?

I have so many questions, but I know I need to wait until tonight to ask what the next step is. I didn't see Maggie after she went to speak with Ben, and I haven't received any emails from human resources, but I still can't say that the coast is clear.

My anxiety is spiraling because I'm not completely sure what is in store for my future. *Did I fuck it all up by falling for my boss? Could I have ignored the feelings that I kept hidden from everyone? Did I just lose the single most important person in my life?*

I leave in a hurry at the end of the day and head straight to Ben's penthouse. I run past the doorman and am granted access to the top floor. When the elevator opens to his foyer, I remove my shoes and drop my purse on the entry table and go in search of Ben.

He's sitting in his library, my favorite place in his home. The lights are dimmed, the fireplace ablaze and he's sitting on the loveseat with a tumbler of whiskey in his hand. His expression is somber. Dread fills my gut as I approach, I can't exactly what's happening and the only sound I can hear is my breathing.

He looks up and places his glass on the side table, then holds out his hand to me. That's all it takes for relief to flood my senses; somehow I know everything will be okay. His eyes hold the relief that I needed and my heart is slamming against my ribcage in happiness. My hand fits in his palm and he pulls me to him. I sit astride him with one of his strong hands on the small of my back while the other runs up the curve of my neck, cradles my jaw, then threads into my hair.

He pulls me to him. "Need you," he whispers against my lips. "I need your kiss."

I let him kiss me. The ocean of feelings in my stomach simmers as our tongues dance together. All thoughts of the problems facing us flee to the back of my mind as my senses take over. He tastes of alcohol and smells like the forest. My hands tug at the hair at his nape as I lean into the kiss further. His hand at my back rounds my ass and his fingers roughly drag to my thigh. He holds me as if he's afraid I will vanish. I press my core against the hardness of his cock and rock against it.

He growls and pulls back slightly, his teeth pulling at my bottom lip.

My hands come to his front and I begin unbuttoning his shirt in haste, needing to have my hands on his skin. Needing the contact to know that this moment is real.

"I'm so in love with you," he says as he runs his lips across the sensitive skin under my ear. "I don't want you to leave me because of this at work."

"I love you too," I declare. "I love you so much. I can't leave you. I won't leave you, ever." I reach in between us and unbuckle his belt.

God damnit, I should have worn a skirt today.

His hands wrap around my wrists and he pulls me away from him. He breaks contact and waits for me to look him in the eyes.

"We should talk. I don't want you to worry right now and have you thinking this is our last time together."

I gasp. "It's not?"

"No. Maggie isn't happy with me right now. She's insisting we update the employee handbook and add rules banning fraternization between staff members. We're going head to head about it, but I won't allow her to let this be the end of you and me. I just can't. Not when I've found love again."

"What if you are asked to step down?" I ask him.

"This is my company. This isn't the Stone Age where it's a taboo thing to date someone that you work with. Times have changed. What we have is completely consensual. Granted, the business climate today is such that there is potential liability with inter-office relationships, but Maggie acknowledged that she never suspected there was anything happening with us, because we kept work and pleasure separate." He smiles playfully. "Mostly."

"See, my stubbornness has paid off."

"Either way, I have a meeting first thing tomorrow morning with Maggie. I would like you to attend with me."

"Am I supposed to?" I ask.

"No. But I would like for you to be by my side. After all, this affects you as well," he says, sincerity plain on his features. I cup his jaw and run my thumb along his chin and up his jawline to his cheek. I smile as I lean in and brush my lips against his. He leans closer and kisses me roughly.

"Ben," I whisper into the kiss.

"I'm not going to let this be the end of us. I can't lose you too," he says, pulling back slightly. "Maggie knows me, she's seen me at my worst and I explained to her what you mean to me. She understands, but I'm sure she may have some proposals in store for us tomorrow. This is not the end of us, I don't want that thought to be in your mind."

CHAPTER THIRTEEN

BENJAMIN

It's too early in the morning for this shit.

Everyone who works here knows I prefer my meetings to be mid-morning and not first thing. But here we are, sitting at the table in my office waiting for Maggie to arrive and start in on us. The air is thick and it's too quiet as Bella and I sit side-by-side.

Maggie walks in and sits opposite us. She places a notepad and a pen in front of her, takes a sip of her coffee, and then looks up at us.

"I carefully considered how to approach this discussion. Isabella, I am glad you are here with us this morning," Maggie starts, politely nodding to Bella.

"Me too," Bella says quietly.

"I want to start out by saying I am extremely happy that Benjamin has found someone. While it's not ideal for that someone to be his direct employee, I think this conversation today can help us come to some agreement on the future with the company and relationships that may pose as a liability for the company."

"Let's hear what you have to say," I say quickly, wanting her to just get on with it.

"I've known you for a long time, Benjamin. I know your character – your *true* character. I also know you were thrown into leading the company and since then you have grown into a force to be reckoned with. You are passionate about this company and the work we do here. You want this company to continue to grow and to flourish and you don't want anything unfortunate to happen to it or your family name. I know that in the recent past we have spoken a few times regarding adding a new section to the employee handbook forbidding employee fraternization, which you declined."

"That's correct." I nod.

"Your father never saw a need for it either. But times have changed since your father led Adams Enterprises. There's a lot more workplace harassment that is talked about these days versus twenty years ago and that is unfortunate that some have felt the need to sweep harassment under the rug so often. There's always that one person who ruins something for everyone else. But it's the harsh truth of the business world as we see it today. I don't want some people to ruin things for others. Or to take advantage of the company policies." She pauses, looking to the both of us.

I speak up. "The last thing I want is for any employee here at Adams Enterprises to have to go through any of those things."

"And that's why our staff is paid based on experience. That's why we have a sexual harassment prevention seminar annually. I'm sure there are other situations where employees have dated one another, but, like your relationship, it's been kept under wraps."

"And we will continue to do so. That was the primary stipulation when we decided to get involved: our personal lives and our professional lives will not mingle."

"I'm afraid that the chain of command here makes it difficult for that to be completely true, you could say something that Isabella may take personally. Or another staffer could flirt with Isabella and you may react to that. We can't predict how either of you would react now that you have personal feelings with one another." Maggie says. I hear Bella gasp and see her wringing her hands a little harder in her lap.

"Now what are you trying to say here? I'm not firing her, and she's not leaving my side," I say to Maggie firmly, my hand reaching to grasp Bella's.

"Benjamin, can you confidently say that you can be objective about the work that Isabella does?" she asks pointedly.

"I can," I say with conviction.

"And Isabella, can you take criticism from Benjamin without thinking its personal?"

"I think the fact that I haven't quit yet indicates that I can, ma'am." Bella holds her head high.

Maggie nods and jots down a few notes on her notepad. She puts her pen down, folds her hands together and sighs.

"What I propose here is written disclosure, which will be added to the handbook. Employees will be required to disclose their romantic relationships with other employees of Adams Enterprises to Human Resources. Having this information up front will help HR determine how to respond appropriately to complaints of harassment, favoritism, or discrimination. The employees will need to sign a contract outlining appropriate behavior. This contract will also include an acknowledgement regarding sexual harassment and will remain in their employee file for the duration of their employment. And for a period of time outlined by the company lawyers after employment."

"And what if staff members are unwilling to sign this relationship contract?" I ask, playing devil's advocate.

"Then we would need to seek either a transfer or termination," Maggie states.

"I think this could be a good compromise. As you know, I don't like telling others what they can and cannot do in their personal lives. With this relationship contract, Adams Enterprises doesn't have to be the bad guy, but can still shield itself from liability related to relationships between employees."

"If I could make a suggestion to the contract, I'm not sure if this would be a standard, but it's worth mentioning. I would think it would be beneficial to include no public displays of affection in the workplace that would make others uncomfortable and if the relationship was to not work out, that no retaliation can occur to one's position within the company," Bella offers.

Maggie nods and smiles. She writes down some more notes and then looks up to the both of us. "That was one of the plans that I wanted to put in place within this change. Thank you Isabella for your thoughts on the matter."

"You two will be the first to sign the contract. If you agree to, of course."

"We will," Bella and I say in unison.

"Marvelous. I will meet with our lawyers and we will draft up contracts. Ben, you will need to look them over and approve. I want to thank the both of you for your time this morning and the professionalism that you both have displayed in this situation. I know personal business in the workplace is not ideal, but I think that we accomplished what I was hoping for." Maggie stands.

"Once you've drafted the wording for the addition to the employee handbook, send that over to Bella when you can so she can add it to one of my daily tasks and have it on my desk for my review." I say as I stand and button my jacket.

Maggie nods and then leaves to go back to her office. Bella

and I turn to each other. We each let out a breath. I walk to sit behind my desk as she takes a seat at one of the chairs in front. She has her notepad in her hand and her pen ready.

"I'm glad that went smoothly," I sigh.

"Me too. I was worried."

"Some businesses ban employee relationships, some overlook them. But I think the route we are taking lets employees feel like adults, like they can make choices as they see fit. I wouldn't want to be the company that forbids it." I fumble with my jacket buttons and pull it off.

"Well, now that that is over, let's get to work." She smiles.

"Such a workaholic." I laugh.

"Well, there are company rules we have to follow, along with our own."

"We haven't signed anything yet," I remind her.

"We've had our own rule from the start of this relationship: *Not at work.*"

"Except that one time," I tease.

"Except that once." She nods with a roll of her eyes.

"And that kiss yesterday."

"Shut up. Let's get to work," she mumbles, crossing her legs over another, poised to start our morning agenda.

CHAPTER FOURTEEN

BENJAMIN

I REVIEWED SEVERAL DRAFTS OF BOTH THE NEW relationship contract and the additions to the employee handbook over the past few weeks. Once I approved everything, Bella and I sat in Maggie's office and signed the first contract. We rolled out the new addition to the handbook and scheduled a seminar. I feel positive that what we're doing is a step forward for the business and in our relationship.

Three weeks after the meeting with Maggie, the relationship between Bella and myself, aside that we're growing closer as we somehow felt that our relationship was no longer something that can be construed as not allowed. We continue to keep our personal lives out of the office and no one notices the small smiles she gives me or the number of times I've checked out her ass when she's walking in front of me, which happens to be eleven times today alone. Not that I'm counting.

I'm walking out of my office for the day when I catch a few other staffers lingering by Bella's door. I quietly stride up behind them and overhear something about happy hour, plenty of guys, and an invitation for Bella to join them. She politely declines and they plead with her to come out.

I've only heard of her going out with one other person – her friend Felipe. Never once in the five months we've been together has she mentioned going out with people from work. So used to being in our bubble, I forget she must have a life outside of me. We aren't together every night, but we are more often than not. I don't want her to feel she can't go out and enjoy herself just because she and I are together.

I clear my throat, making my presence known. The women in front of the door freeze and their eyes go wide as they notice it is me.

"Good evening, Mr. Adams," A short brunette with her hair up and glasses says quietly.

"Ladies," I acknowledge them. "I need to speak with Isabella before I leave."

They scatter quickly as if I've frightened them. I turn to Bella and smile.

"Was that necessary?" She eyes me.

"Probably not. Go out with them tonight. I plan to go to the gym and then I have my monthly dinner plans."

"I'm not feeling like it. I was planning on just going home tonight."

"Go. Socialize," I urge her.

"You sure?" she asks, her interest piqued. "I was think of coming over tonight."

"My Bella, I don't want to hold you in my castle like you're under lock and key. I know you rarely go out; I know I hog your time. I don't want you to get bored with our relationship, to feel like you don't do anything outside of us."

"Just so you know, I wasn't *not* going because of you," she says.

"I know."

"As long as you know that, Mr. Adams." She crosses her arms.

"I would love to kiss that defiance right out of your mouth right now," I tease her.

"Too bad you can't." She smiles a wicked smile and winks.

"Tauntress. I'll see you tonight then?" I ask, lingering in the doorway.

"If you're lucky." She picks at her nails, acting as if she's not affected by me.

"Oh, I'm feeling lucky." I rap my knuckles on the doorway twice and wink at her as I exit and head towards the elevators. I turn to face her once in the elevator and she's already on the phone, likely calling her co-workers to tell them she changed her mind. She waves at me and I press the down button.

CHAPTER FIFTEEN

BELLA

"I can't believe this is the first time you've come out with us! I could have sworn we've invited you before," Tina, the brunette with glasses, exclaims before she takes a large gulp of her colorful drink.

I toy with the straw of my mojito and smile. "You guys have, I just haven't had time. I figured that I should start getting out though. So, here I am!"

"Cheers to that!" Tina says, holding up her drink. She and I clink glasses as two others from work join us.

"Bella. You have to tell us everything about you. You work for Mr. Adams; is he as scary as he seems to be?" Megan, the blonde, asks.

"He is. But I've learned how to manage him and his moods." I smile, then take a sip of my drink. *Oh, this is good.* I take another sip and smile.

"Lucky girl. He is one gorgeous specimen, even if he's a complete animal. I wouldn't mind letting him sink his claws into me." Megan gushes, as she leans in closer.

I fight the urge to get territorial and to lash out with jealousy. Instead, I take another sip of my drink.

"Oh, please. You have enough with your *affair* with Micah." Tina rolls her eyes. Micah is one of the directors in the software department. I thought he was happily married.

"Yeah, but now there's that new policy and he doesn't want to sign the stupid love contract, in fear of his boss finding out."

"Or that your affair would be frowned on by HR since he's cheating on his wife and he might not be considered as someone with a good head on his shoulders," I add mindlessly.

"Exactly, that!" Tina points at me.

"I think the policy was created because someone – maybe it was Micah – couldn't keep his pen in his pocket and instead wanted to sample the company ink," Tina explains.

"I know there was no policy previously, so maybe it was just time," I defend.

"Something had to have sparked the interest of management. Didn't you attend the gala earlier this year with Mr. Adams? Maybe that was it." I can practically see the light bulb come on over her head. "Hold the phone a minute here, is something happening between you and Mr. Adams?" Megan covers her mouth in shock.

I laugh it off, feeling the effects of my drink. "I was his date because he forgot to get one. It was a work thing; really, that's all it was."

"Maybe the gala is the reason then." Tina nods.

"The policy didn't come across Ben's— I mean, Mr. Adams' desk until recently though. So, I doubt it."

"There are so many conspiracies here. Oh, I'm empty." Megan frowns, looking at the cup in her hand. "I want another drink!" She switches topics as she waves her hand in the air to catch the attention of the waiter. She bats her eyes and orders us another round of drinks before I can decline.

I stumble into the foyer once the elevator door opens, nearly crashing into the entry table. I drop my shoes, which I removed in the car ride over here, and hold onto the wall for support as I set off to locate Ben.

I giggle as thoughts from the night run hazily through my head. I bump into a framed picture on a wall and snort loudly.

"Hey, picture. Sorry," I say through a fit of giggles. I try to right myself and continue down the hallway.

When did this hallway get so long? I get to the first doorway and remember that it's a bathroom. I pause in the doorway, holding onto both sides. *Did I need to go to the bathroom? What am I doing here?* I shrug and enter the bathroom, not sure how long I was in there or if I did anything. Either way, I flush and wash my hands. I look at the mirror in front of me and there is two of me, possibly three. I try to fix my hair, but give up and put it in a messy bun instead and then leave the confines of the small room.

I exit to the left and when I reach the picture on the wall again, I realize I went the wrong way and turn around to head in the direction of the bedroom. Again.

I continue to use the wall to guide me all the way to Ben's room. Once I am there, I feel relieved. I disrobe as I cross the room, leaving a trail of clothes on the floor, then crawl from the foot of the bed to his side. Ben wakes to the sudden movement and my clumsy attempts to nestle against him.

He brushes the hair away from my face and I think he smiles at me. I'm not sure. Up close, right now, he's blurry. But I can smell the spearmint toothpaste he uses and I smile.

"I can tell you had fun," he comments.

"I had some, yes." I slur. I know I'm slurring.

"Maybe too much fun?"

"There's nothing of a sort." I hiccup.

"Let me grab you some water and aspirin and get you to sleep, yeah?" His tone is soothing.

"Okays." I close my eyes and snuggle into the pillow.

Moments later, I wake to my shoulder being shaken. Ben holds out a glass and pills to me, pushing them closer when my eyes open a bit more. I lean up on my elbows and take the glass from him. I open my mouth and Ben smiles as he places the pills on my tongue. I chug the water and then hand the glass back to him.

"Sank you," I mumble and lie back down, succumbing to sleep. I feel Ben get back into bed beside me and pull me to him. That's the last thing I notice until morning.

CHAPTER SIXTEEN

BENJAMIN

BELLA IS LIGHTLY SNORING BESIDE ME IN THE MORNING when I wake. She's curled up with one of her knees up to her chest. Half of the blankets are kicked off of her, and her arms are clutching the half of her pillow she is laying on. Her clothes are scattered all over the bedroom floor and she's comfortably naked. Her mouth is slightly open, and her hair covers most of her face. I go through the motions to get ready for work and wait until the last minute to wake her up.

I rub her shoulder and sit down beside her. She takes a moment before she opens her eyes and when she focuses on me, she looks surprised.

"What? How? Huh?" She fumbles for words.

"How do you feel?" I ask her quietly.

"Like I pretended that I was binge drinking last night. How did I get here?" she asks, confused. She sits up slowly, rubbing her forehead and squinting her eyes.

"I'm not entirely sure, but I'm hoping you got a ride some-how," I say. "Are you up for work today, or are you calling in?"

"What time is it?" She looks at the clock. "Not that I'm

trying to take advantage of our relationship or anything, but can I come in an hour or two late?"

"Of course, party animal," I tease her, then kiss her forehead. "I'm going to get out of here. See you at the office. Take your time."

"Thank you." She smiles as she melts back into my bed. I turn and look at her before I leave. She's draped her arm over her eyes, her mouth is agape, and she's already snoring again.

She couldn't be more beautiful.

I set a house system reminder to wake her up gently in an hour, and leave her a note fixed to the panel beside the elevator.

IT'S NOON WHEN BELLA COMES IN. SHE LOOKS FRESH, AS IF she hadn't been completely drunk last night. She comes into my office once she settles in and sits in front of my desk. I'm on the phone with Ryder, discussing schedules, so she waits quietly.

"Bella will make sure to contact Naomi this afternoon. I would like the two of them to work closely together if you can allow for that?" I smile at Bella while I listen to Ryder boast about how he's willing to do whatever he needs.

"Great. I'll have her get in touch. I've got to run; someone important just walked into my office."

We say our goodbyes and then I give Bella my undivided attention. She smiles at me, but I can tell by how the smile doesn't reach her eyes that it's lacking enthusiasm.

"You could have stayed in bed all day. I would survive," I say, leaning back in my chair.

"That's not very adult of me. I shouldn't have drank so much last night."

"Why did you drink so much then?"

"It was more so a way for me to keep busy. The girls kept

bringing up relationships, or you, and I would take a sip instead and feign disinterest."

"They'd bring me up? Why?"

"Because you're the big bad boss. An animal. And a hot commodity. The general consensus is that, while you are a complete dick, you are very desirable. Women like an asshole sometimes." She shrugs.

"Are you saying that I'm not?" I tease her.

"Oh, you are. I just had to cage my jealousy last night. It was hard."

"And booze was the key." I nod, understanding why she got so drunk.

"On a side note, Micah from Software is cheating on his wife," she says quietly.

"Oh, that's not news. He's likely hooked up with half of his staff."

"Ew, gross." She crinkles her nose.

"Who is it now?" I ask, curiously.

"Megan," she whispers.

"I don't know a Megan." I shake my head.

"She's blonde, works in IT. An admin, I think."

"His wife finds out about all the affairs and she gets back at him by doing the pool boy or something. It's a game they play. An eye for an eye," I disclose.

"Why don't they just get divorced?"

"Neither of them believe in it, I suppose. I'm not sure. I do my best to stay out of other people's personal stuff."

"This new company relationship contract, he won't sign it."

"He would have to sign one regularly with the revolving door he has."

"Is there anything that can be done?" she asks with hope.

"I'll talk to Maggie. She should be aware of his extracurriculars. We did mention that we would have to do transfers or even terminations in situations like this."

"I just don't want him to be the cause of another policy going into effect and potentially affecting us."

"I won't let that happen. Now, let's talk about work. I feel like we're breaking the rules here," I say, trying to get us back on track.

"It's my fault. I'm not myself today." She straightens her posture and taps her notepad with her pen." Okay, bossman, hit me!"

I give her the contact information for the collaboration with Ryder Tech and give her some small tasks to do for research to fill her day. Once we're finished, I head to HR and check in with Maggie about Micah. I'm more than a little annoyed that I'm being forced to abide by this new rule and others are ignoring it.

A few hours later, Maggie comes into my office and shuts the door behind her.

"Micah states that he is not currently having any relationships outside of his marriage. We can't specifically prove that he is without indicting Bella on her outing with the girl who he is supposedly sleeping with," she says. "At this point, it's construed as gossip, and we have no actual evidence."

"Transfer Megan to another department, maybe?" I ask.

"Right now it's a he said/she said game. Gossip, there's no need to take any further action with this."

"Did he ask you why the subject came up?"

"No, he told me that since the policy went into effect, he's been faithful to his wife. He acted put off by the questions, but I had to explain that I was just following up on someone's report."

"This is why I initially didn't want this kind of policy. I hate being caught up in people's business." I groan as I roll my head, cracking my neck.

"I can understand that. But think of it as protection for your business."

"I know, I know. So, if anyone reports an unsigned relationship to HR, then you issue a warning, correct?"

"It's not so cut and dry. First, we would complete an investigation by interviewing the parties involved. Once we complete the investigation, with the interviews with the parties, then we can determine a method of action. That is language in the handbook now, so I will follow that protocol." She nods as she stands.

"I still don't like this, Maggie." I want to pull out my hair in frustration.

"I know you don't. But it's a smart move, Ben. It protects the company and its employees." She leaves and I know that she's right. I need to think about the long term and not just the here and now.

CHAPTER SEVENTEEN

BENJAMIN

BELLA IS SITTING WITH HER LEGS TUCKED UNDER HER reading a book in my library. I'm sitting opposite her in my leather chair, pretending to read when all I really want to do is to ravish her.

"Ben. You're growling," she says, not looking up from her book.

"I am?" I ask.

"You are. Stop it, I'm trying to read."

I put my book down beside me and advance on her. I sit beside her, then move her hair to her shoulder and kiss the column of her neck. Goosebumps rise after each kiss and I see her body visibly quake from my touch.

"I want you," I say in her ear as I lightly breathe across her skin before sucking her earlobe into my mouth.

"You're so distracting." She laughs as she puts her book down and moves to face me. My hand cups her jaw and pulls her mouth to connect with mine. Our tongues move against ONE another, dipping in and out of our joined mouths as our kisses deepen. She turns fully and crawls onto my lap. My hands roam her back, underneath her shirt with up and down motions over the span of her silky skin. I unclasp her bra and lift her shirt. She accommodates my advances and soon is sitting topless on my lap. Seeing her delicate skin bare before me makes my fingers itch to touch her, while my cock is achingly aware of the proximity of her center.

I bend my head and kiss the top of her breast as my hands move to cup them. I squeeze them and pull her nipple into my mouth. I roll the peak around with my tongue as it pebbles and use my teeth to pull as I release her breast and move to the other, repeating the same pattern. She arches into me as my teeth graze her and her core is pressed against my hardness as she rocks against my length.

"I love it when you sit on me like this, when you ride my cock and use me for your own pleasure. I love it when your tits are in my face and I can suck on one as you slide up and down on me. Do you like that too, baby?" I growl into her mouth as I plant kisses in between breaths.

"God, yes! Yes, Ben. I love all of that!" she moans, grinding on my cock.

"I want you to show me. Show me how much you like to ride my cock."

Quick breaths blow out from her mouth and her chest heaves. She pulls back from me and places her hands on my shoulders as she stands. Instantly, my lap goes cold. She unbuttons her pants and pulls them down. Next, her fingers hook the sides of her panties and she slowly takes them off, bending slowly and then stands, baring all to me.

There's wetness on her thighs and I can see her excitement as she kneels down between my legs and reach for my pants. She pulls out my cock and strokes me. She leans in and licks me from base to tip as my body quivers from her touch. I lean my head back and lightly groan. Her tongue swirls over the head of my cock before she sucks me down her throat, causing my body to jerk. I pull her off and pierce her with my eyes.

"I said I wanted you to ride me. While I love it when my cock is in your mouth, nothing compares to your pussy."

"Such a beast." She smiles and places her knees on either side of my legs as she lines herself up with my cock and then plants herself.

She fits perfectly. She is perfect. She was made for me.

Her hips rock back and forth as I dip my head as my tongue reaches out to lavish her breasts once more. She moves on me and mewls in satisfaction as we get lost in each other.

She is the light in my darkness. I wasn't supposed to need anyone anymore, but I fucking need her. She makes me bearable.

"I love getting lost in you," she moans.

I can feel the pulsing of her pussy. Our breaths come in short gasps as we move with each other. My hips surge up and forward with her motions.

She controls the rhythm, the movement and my heart. I'm tamed, no longer out of control. She's quelled my animal instincts and made me a man again.

I fucking love her.

She tells me she's coming as her body begins to tremble from her orgasm, and I start to release into her. It feels amazing when we come together. She milks my cock and brings me to my ultimate high.

CHAPTER EIGHTEEN

BENJAMIN

I AM SICK AND TIRED OF TALKING ABOUT RELATIONSHIPS, especially other people's relationships, the potential problems office relationships can create, and the politics of whether or not an employee will be forthcoming about their relationships with other staff. I hate getting involved in other people's business because no one needs to up in mine.

For the third week in a row, Maggie has brought up new concerns over the number of people who have come to her to fill out a contract regarding their relationship. I keep telling her I do not need to know the details, yet she still brings them to my attention. The number is miniscule compared to the thousands of individuals this company employs, but to Maggie and her team this new policy is overwhelming.

"Maggie. What do you need from me? What do you need me to do to make this easier on you?" I ask.

She looks taken aback by my offer. "Well, um... I wasn't prepared for you to ask something like that, Ben. I think we need... hmmm...." She taps her forefinger to her chin and looks up at the ceiling. "We have a budget for a temporary staff member for a few weeks to input and create these new files for the contracts, I would like to get someone to help me out. I'm up to my head in paperwork and I fear drowning."

"I think we can do that. I don't want to add any additional tasks onto your already busy work-load with this new project we've got going."

"It would be entry level, but obviously with the sensitive information he/she would be handling, not just a kid off the street."

"Roger that. Do you have anything else? I have to head downstairs to check on a project."

"No. Thank you, Ben. Really. Thank you." Maggie smiles as she gets up.

I follow behind her and stop at the door. "I'll have Bella look into the budgets and once she reports back to me, I'll find you."

Maggie nods and we head in different directions as I head to Bella's office to relay to her what I need. I haven't seen her all morning, since we both arrived to the office. But with the new project, she has been out of the office meeting with Naomi and getting the teams what they need.

This new project will bring home technology to a new standard. If all works well, each home will be more than a smart home, but a smart everything: energy conservation, adaptable to climate change and surroundings, and best of all, connected to the homeowner's network while maintaining stringent security so that all their information is protected. Teaming up with Ryder Tech, while we have competed on previous projects, was the smartest idea I think I've ever come up with.

I leave a note for Bella and consider texting her. Instead, I hope I run into her on the team floor where they're working on everything.

We chose my offices, as I have clean environments on two levels, whereas Ryder only has one zone dedicated to clean environments. I had the extra space at the moment, and it was my idea, so my building is the home base.

I go downstairs and check in with everyone. I speak to a few of the team leaders and get an idea of where they are currently with everything. We're still in the beginning stages, and while plans have been created, there is still a lot going on. In the corner of the lab, a 3D printer is creating a house, which I assume will be used for examples.

I smile at what we have created so far and continue to look around.

I stop when I see Naomi standing alone with a clipboard and her pen in her hand. I look around the area and still don't see Bella. As I approach, her face reddens and she quickly looks away.

"Hello, Naomi. Have you seen Isabella?" I ask her.

"She was supposed to be here. Someone told me when I got here that she went out to pick up some supplies and food, but I haven't seen her or heard from her all morning."

That's strange. She's not flakey by any means and she's usually very good at communicating her whereabouts to everyone.

I check my phone and see no messages from her. I pull up her last text to me and I quickly type something out to her as I thank Naomi and continue walking the floor.

My phone vibrates in my pocket. Bella's number appears on the screen and I smile as I slide to answer her call.

"Well, where have you escaped off to?" I say teasingly.

"Hello, this is Nurse Erikman from Hollybrooke United Hospital. This phone was on the person who is my patient. I assume you are a relative, or spouse?"

"Yes." I croak, my throat suddenly dry.

"Good. Mr...?"

"Adams. Benjamin Adams," I rasp.

"Mr. Adams. Isabella was in a motor vehicle accident. She was just moved into the ICU after surgery and is currently in critical, but stable, condition."

"I'm on my way," I say and hang up as I get into the elevator.

My mind is racing in a thousand directions. I dial for my driver and wait for him at the curb. While I wait, I call Maggie and inform her of the situation and indicate that I'll follow up on what we spoke about when I have a chance. She offered to come with me, but I declined. I need to see Bella, by myself. I need to make sure she's all right, to see her with my own eyes and confirm she is okay.

She lies still in the hospital bed with tubes and machines surrounding her. Her area has an eerie silence interrupted only by the constant beeps of the machines and monitors. One of the machines breathes for her, another machine is providing her fluids, wires are hooked up to her in all sorts of places and even though there is constant beeping, there's a thickness in the room. Her face, her neck, and her arms are blotchy and bruised.

I feel so helpless. The lights are dim, but bright enough to burn my eyes as I fight off the range of emotions that I'm feeling. I sit in the chair beside her bed with my head in my hands. I feel like I'm having deja vu. I shake my head and fall back into the chair beside her bed.

The room is bright and smells like hand sanitizer. Renae is motionless in the hospital bed, hooked up to wires that connect to hospital machines.

These machines are keeping her alive until her mother arrives.

"Brain dead," the doctor said, his voice full of apology. "She

and Mr. Hunter – her boyfriend – were speeding down the highway and were stuck by another vehicle. Her boyfriend was taken in an ambulance as well, but we believe he was discharged with non-life-threatening injuries. He said he would be right back, but that was hours ago. Who are you again?"

I clear my throat. "Family." I'm not sure if that's the right answer right now, but the rest I will have to sort out later.

Not even a year ago, I sat in this very hospital saying goodbye to my ex. Now I have to do the same to her.

A uniformed police officer knocks on the window, breaking me out of my past. I stand to greet him.

"I'm Officer Simon. Mr. Adams, I presume?" He shakes my offered hand and then motions to the chairs against the wall near the door.

I nod, then clear my throat. "What happened?"

"Ms. Dubois's vehicle was struck head on by another vehicle. The airbags deployed, but it appears that there seems to have been a malfunction. The individual of the other vehicle attempted to flee the scene; however, he is in our custody at the moment. The act appeared to be intentional based upon the scene and the actions of the suspect." He pauses and clears his throat. "We would like for you to come down to the station when you can to see if you can ID the suspect," he states. "I am hoping that you would be able to identify the suspect and hopefully you'll be able to provide us with information pertaining to our investigation."

"You can't ID him?"

"He's not speaking, he had no identification on his person when we picked him up, and his fingerprints are not in our system."

"No facial recognition matches coming up with DMV searches?"

"That can take too long. If you know who he is, that's a hell of a lot quicker."

I nod with understanding.

"Let me speak with the nurse and make sure that they have my number in case she wakes up."

Moments later, I'm walking through the hospital flanked by two police men on the way to their patrol car outside. We arrive at their station and I'm directed to a viewing room. Officer Simon stays with me as the door on the other side of the two-way glass opens. A man, dressed in all black walks in, his head is hanging down, stringy dark brown hair shielding his features, which appear to have dirt all over them. He keeps his head down as he's moved by the policeman to the seat at the table. The officer takes the man's hands and pulls them up to handcuff him to the eyelet in the center of the table. The man's head is still down.

"Was he injured in the accident at all?" I ask, not taking my eyes off of him. He seems familiar, but I can't be sure until I see his face.

"Miraculously, not as bad considering the damage seen on the vehicles. His airbags deployed, he has some bruising but his injuries are minor." Officer Simon says as he reaches to the button to turn on the speaker so we can hear what's being said on the other side of the wall.

"—we need to know what your plan was with striking the other vehicle as you did." The voice of the officer facing the suspect says with a stern tone through the speaker.

The man's head stays down and he says nothing. His demeanor isn't of one of is fear or defiance. His posture just portrays him as unaffected, as though he's there but not.

"Can the officer ask him to lift his head?" I request.

"Since we got here, he's been like this. He shut down upon

stepping foot in the station it seems. We had to have someone hold his head up for his mug shot."

"Can I see the mug shot? I don't want to be here any longer than I need to, in case Bella wakes up. I want to be by her side."

"Understood. Give me a minute, and I'll go grab that for you."

While Officer Simon is gone, I continue listening to the officer in the other room try to get the guy to talk. Nothing is working; the guy is silent and unmoving.

I observe what I can of him to try to place him. His shoulders, his neck, his hands. He's familiar and it's pissing me off that I cannot place him. I'm gritting my teeth, angry at myself and at the man in the other room. When the officer comes back in, he hands me the tablet with a photo on it and I look down.

I feel light-headed and feel my knees give out on me before I hit the ground.

My vision goes dark.

CHAPTER NINETEEN

BELLA

I'M STUCK IN A HAZE. NOTHING HERE SEEMS PERMANENT AND *I'm not coming into contact with any fixtures as I slowly walk through the haze. I can't make out any smells or sounds, aside from the faint beeping off in the distance.*

I don't know where I am, and I feel nothing.

Should I be feeling something?

What happened?

Where am I?

I close my eyes and stop walking. I take a deep breath, hoping for the smells of the city, the sounds of people to fill my senses.

But nothing.

Just haze.

How did I get here?

CHAPTER TWENTY

BENJAMIN

My eyes open slowly and I'm surrounded by people in uniforms. Immediately, I try to sit up, but a strong arm is on my chest and a voice tells me to take it slow. A face comes into view, an EMT with shaggy brown hair and two-days of scruff is kneeling beside me on the ground. He smiles when my eyes focus on him and he holds up his tiny flashlight and shines it into my eyes. He looks up and nods to someone who then also kneels down and comes into my view.

"Mr. Adams, you gave me quite the scare. How are you feeling?" he asks me.

"How... How long was I out?" I stutter.

"A few minutes. You basically buckled once I handed you the tablet."

The tablet. Yes, the tablet with his face. His Face.

"Where is he?" I say, my voice a little louder than before. Suddenly all I feel is rage as I get to my feet and wobble a bit.

"Whoa, take it easy there, buddy," the EMT says as he grasps my shoulders. "You need to move slowly right now, until your equilibrium catches up to you."

I grimace at him and he backs away.

"The tablet?" I ask Officer Simon who comes up beside me. He turns to one of the other officers and holds out his hand. The tablet is placed in his hands and he unlocks it, then enters into their database.

"Let me pull up the file. Ah, there it is. I take it you know him?" He hands me the tablet again with the mug shot on the screen.

"His name," I say slowly, my anger boiling, "is Elliot Hunter."

"And you are sure about that?" Officer Simon asks.

"As sure about his name as I am about my own. We were college roommates, best friends at the time. He was involved in a car accident with my fiancée ten years ago, a car accident that killed her," I say with conviction.

Officer Simon nods and leaves the room. He returns a moment later and holds his hand out to me. I take his hand in mine and grasp it as we shake.

"I'm deeply sorry that you are having to deal with this. With your identification, we'll make sure we hold him. We need your company to file a loss report, and take down any information that we can."

"I will have someone from my office call you to do the report. I would like to get back to the hospital now, if I can."

He nods in understanding.

"I'll be in touch. Here's my card, call me and I'll give you any updates I can. I'll be in contact with the hospital too, and well, we'll need to get Ms. Dubois's statement when she is able."

I take a cab back to the hospital and hope, just hope that she wakes when I get there. Her being asleep is killing me and now the fact that I know that Elliot Hunter, of all people, caused this to happen has my blood boiling again.

Why would he purposely cause this accident? What does he have to gain from this?

I walk into the hospital and make my way to the ICU and find her room empty. In a panic, I rush to the nurses' station.

"Her lungs collapsed. She was rushed into surgery about five minutes ago."

"Why didn't anyone call me?" I yell.

"Sir. Please calm down. We only just now received an update on her status. We cannot give incomplete information. This is me telling you right now. I'm sorry, but that's protocol."

I simmer down and take a deep breath. "I'm sorry. This hasn't been the greatest of days."

"I know, sir, and for that I'm greatly sorry. Unfortunately, since she's not in her room, you'll have to wait in the waiting room just outside those doors. The doctor or one of the surgery nurses will come out and update you soon. I'll inform them you're here."

"I can't lose her," I mumble.

"The doctors and nurses on her team are some of the best. She's in good hands." The nurse rounds the station and guides me to the waiting room. She squeezes my shoulder and then turns to leave.

After a few moments of sitting in the uncomfortable chair sorting through feelings of anger and helplessness, I pull out my phone.

"Mrs. Rosemary," I croak into the phone.

I tell her everything. I pour out my heart as if she were my mother. She listens and adds in encouraging words when I break for a breath. She confirms that she will make sure the company vehicle loss report is completed by calling the office. I ask her to get me contact information for Bella's parents and then we hang up. Minutes later, my cell phone chimes with a message that includes a phone number. I place the call to her family and relay all the information to her mother over the phone. With her mother's tears and words of encouragement weighing heavy on my heart, I sit in the waiting room, unsure of what will happen to my Bella, pissed off and questioning the reasons why all this has happened.

I'm not sure how long I wait for someone to come and update me. It could have been minutes or hours. Time has become lost to me.

My shoulder is nudged and someone sits beside me.

Mrs. Rosemary. There's worry in her eyes, and silent questions.

"Is she... Is she okay?" she asks, her chin quivering.

"I'm still waiting," I reply as a doctor walks up to us.

"The family for Ms. Dubois?" he asks.

I stand and prepare myself for the worst.

"Thankfully, we caught the problem right away and Ms. Dubois is back in her room. She suffered from a traumatic pneumothorax, her lungs were collapsed in the accident and we went in and sealed any of the leaks of her lung closed. It appears that she had the collapsed lungs at the onset of her arriving, but somehow the first operation didn't seal all the punctures. She will have a chest tube in for a few days, until her chest expands. But from what I can see, she's out of the woods."

"And her other injuries?" I ask.

"According to her chart, she will heal normally. She had some initial internal bleeding when she was first brought in by the Aid Car. She has, as you've seen several contusions and some fractures. There was a nurse checking her bags at the moment her heart rate accelerated and she started coding, so immediate action was taken. She was very lucky. We are going to admit her to one of the regular rooms in twenty four hours, should she continue to progress and once she's breathing on her own. The nurses in the ICU will continue to observe her and then we'll set her up on the fourth floor," he replied.

"Thank God," Mrs. Rosemary says from beside me.

"Do you have any other questions?" the doctor asks me.

"Can I see her?"

"Give her until she gets upstairs. Grab something to eat. I'll make sure the nurses come to get when she's moved."

"Thank you, doctor," I say, extending my hand.

While a commotion at the front door distracts me, the doctor turns on his heel and leaves. Mrs. Rosemary and I observe a rumpled couple rush into the room looking frantic. Upon closer observation, the woman looks like a shorter and older Bella and I clue in that they must be her parents.

I stand to my full height, brush flat my shirt, and take a deep breath.

"Mr. and Mrs. Dubois?" I ask as their eyes meet mine.

With a sigh of relief, they come to stand before me. Introductions are made and I give them the good news that the doctor just gave us as well as introduce them to Mrs. Rosemary.

Mrs. Rosemary. She's here, not as my employee, but as a concerned friend. She was concerned over me as well as Bella and came to be by my side when I didn't even ask. I am grateful for her presence.

I look over at her, talking with Bella's mom and smile. She's the closest thing I have to a parent. She's known me since forever. She takes care of me, even though I think I've tried to fire her several times, saying I could take care of myself. She's here, talking to my girlfriend's parents and boasting about Bella.

I smile for the first time today and feel so relieved that I sit back down in the chair and pass out.

CHAPTER TWENTY-ONE

BELLA

THE HAZE IS GONE, AND ALL I FEEL IS PAIN.

Excruciating pain.

Every part of me is in pain and I just want to cry out. I slowly open my eyes to a ceiling that doesn't look familiar.

My eyes burn, and I feel like my skin is crawling from the inside out. I open my mouth, but no sounds come out.

Beeping. The beeps sound like the beeps from the haze, but louder and more frequent.

I hear a series of beeps and slowly voices separate out of the din. I gingerly turn my head and see Ben standing there pressing a button. He then leans over me carefully and brushes hair off of my forehead.

"Hi, my beauty. I can't tell you how happy I am to see those beautiful blue eyes look up at me," he says, his eyes moist.

I open my mouth and he shakes his head.

"Wait for the doctors to check you over. It may hurt to talk," he tells me softly. I nod, a tear forming at the corner of my eye, as another man comes into view. He's a stranger, but I assume is a doctor based upon his white coat.

He checks all my vitals. He motions for the nurse standing at the door to come in and they begin to pull the tube from my throat. I cough at the sudden burn as the doctor pulls his chair up to me. He continues to check on me, my fluids and whatever he's looking at on his tablet.

Ben is standing behind him, and he smiles at me. I can see his smile is strained but he's trying.

"Isabella. You were in a head-on collision. When you came in you had a TBI, which meant we had to go in and relieve the pressure around your brain. You had internal bleeding, a broken arm and several broken ribs. You spent the majority of your morning in the ICU until your lungs collapsed, likely from damage due to one of your broken ribs. Your serious injuries have been repaired, but for a few days, you'll have this chest tube in to equalize everything." The doctor finishes as he hands me a whiteboard. "It will hurt to speak because we had to intubate you, but these ice chips should help build up the moisture and the soreness of your throat. Take your time with speaking; I imagine that you're in a lot of pain right now from all of this. The button right here" —He points to the remote beside my head.— "this is for pain. It's regulated, so you can't overdose on the medication, of course, this is a controlled release system. Now, I know that's a lot of information, but do you have any questions for me?"

"I have a question," a booming voice says from the other side of the room. I slowly turn my head and see my dad stand up and come to my bedside. He smiles down at me and takes my hand. "Hi, pumpkin," he says, his tone softening for me.

"Yes, sir. What can I answer for you?" The doctor turns to my dad.

"Why didn't the doctors notice her lungs were affected by the broken ribs during the first surgery? Ben tells me she had two surgeries," he scolds.

"At the time of the first surgery, just after she was first brought in, there were minor signs of lung deflation, the punctures were sealed but either a new puncture formed or the doctor missed one in his tests. We will be having someone look into the situation. The lungs re-collapsed several hours later while a nurse was in her room completing some of her routine checks when she noticed the indications of her condition. She was rushed into emergency surgery immediately."

"Honey, relax. Isabella is here, she's awake. She's okay." My mom comes into view and wraps her arm around Dad, then peers down at me with a warm smile. Her other hand rubs along my hairline.

The doctor's voice interrupts. "If that will be all, we will need to notify the police that Isabella has woken up. They want to interview her about the accident."

"Thank you, doctor," Mom says.

The room is quiet except for the machines humming and the monitoring of my heartbeat. Ben comes back into my view.

"So, this wasn't the way I was expecting to meet your parents." He smiles.

I return his smile, or at least I think I do.

"Once you get better, we'll need to speak about your communication skills. We didn't even know you were dating someone, especially someone like Ben," Mom gushes.

I want to crawl under the blanket but moving isn't pleasant. I slowly point to the ice chips and my mother rushes to give them to me. After I've slowly chewed several, I attempt to speak. The doctor was right, it does hurt, but I power through.

"What the hell happened?" I rasp out, looking to Ben.

I see a swirl of fury in his eyes.

"Elliot Hunter," he simply states.

"Your old friend? The one who...?" I let my question trail off purposely as Ben nods.

"I went down to the police station not too long after I first came to the hospital and it was him."

I want to cry, I can't imagine the amount of pain that he's feeling right now. I've never had any additional contact with that man aside from the time where Ben kicked him out of his office.

Why would he target me?

CHAPTER TWENTY-TWO

BENJAMIN

Officer Simon came and spoke with Bella an hour after she started talking. She was clearly in pain with every movement she attempted to make. It pained me to see her like that.

He also shared the latest developments regarding Elliot. Seem once he knew the cops had identified him, he began talking. He blamed me for ruining his life. Because of my parents' deaths and being forced to start a new life, he wasn't able to come up with the capital to start the business we were planning on his own, so he never really had a stable career. He had schemes and dreams, or whatever he would call them, and sought out heavy hitters to invest, but nothing ever came to fruition. He believed I'd black-balled him to other companies, which was not the case. I didn't think about him. He also felt that, since his great love died all those years ago, I didn't deserve to have one, and that's the reason behind the car accident.

Somewhere in his messed-up head, that made sense to him.

It makes no sense to me.

The general consensus of the room, among Bella, her

parents, and me was to press charges for attempted manslaughter. But since the charge is so hefty, I couldn't make the decision, the district attorney would. As the officer was leaving, he asked to speak to me.

"Mr. Hunter has lawyered up," he warns. "Between you and me, he doesn't show a modicum of remorse," Officer Simon says.

"Not surprised."

"I'm sorry this all happened to you. I can't even imagine the day you've had," he says.

"It feels like today has been several." I palm the back of my neck.

"Take it easy, and I'll be in touch."

We shake hands and go our separate ways.

A FEW WEEKS AFTER THE ACCIDENT, HER ROOM HAD become full of flowers, balloons, and stuffed animals, and I had a pile of paperwork about after care instructions, follow up appointments, and insurance forms. About that same time, Bella was allowed to leave the hospital. Rather than having her go to her home, I made sure she was set up at the penthouse, just in case.

Her chest tube was removed since she vastly improved two days later and she participated in a few days of breathing exercises and routine checks for the remainder of the time she was hospitalized.

Once her parents were assured I would take good care of her, they left. Meeting the parents wasn't bad under the circumstances, but we promised a proper introduction once Bella was better.

We've spoken with the detective over the weeks and he

keeps us abreast of what's going on with Elliot and his attorney. The district attorney's office is going for everything Elliot has, for attempted murder. based upon the evidence that they had as well as his police statements.

It took Bella three months to fully recover from all her injuries. I refused to allow her to come back to the office, and as a result I was all over the place when I was there. I realized in the time she was on medical leave that I am a totally unorganized person. I'm grateful for her in so many ways that I doubt I could ever properly communicate it to her. While Bella was on leave, I kept to myself. I became a recluse and focused solely on work and making sure Bella was okay. Mrs. Rosemary took care of Bella while I was at work during the day and sometimes late into the night if I had to be at the office.

Mrs. Rosemary and I never spoke about her coming to the hospital the day of Bella's accident. But she is aware of how appreciative I am that she was there with me. I tried to broach the subject once we were home and she shushed me and went about her business. I feel she is an adoptive parent, and I can't help but be thankful my parents brought her into our lives.

All I want is to put the accident and Elliot Hunter out of my mind, but that didn't happen until the case was over. Bella had to testify on the stand about what she remembered from the moment she left the office to when she woke in the hospital room.

I won't ever unhear her testimony. It bolstered the fact that the accident was meant for an intended victim. His apartment proved that he watched Bella with her comings and goings. There were timelines and descriptions all over his place. He had several different scenarios planned out. The look on Elliot's face further confirmed my thoughts.

CHAPTER TWENTY-THREE

BELLA

I SIT ON THE STAND; MY HANDS ARE FOLDED IN MY LAP AND I wait for the orders of Ben's attorney for me to relay the events of my day of the accident as over time the moments have come back to me, while fragmented – I can remember the majority of the events.

"I left the office with the intent to pick up supplies and a breakfast order for our special teams project that Adams Enterprises and Ryder Tech had teamed up on. I was at a red light in the left lane waiting for my turn to go. Once the light turned green, the car going opposite of me turned into my lane and accelerated across the middle section right into the vehicle I was in," I recall the events. "Then I woke up in the hospital."

"How are you sure that the car was coming for you specifically?" the attorney asked.

"The way he swerved into what was my lane. He lined his car up with mine perfectly, there is no question it wasn't an accident." I reply.

"And did you get a good look at the individual when his vehicle was coming towards yours?"

"It happened so fast, that honestly I did not. I was braking and panicking as I was boxed in by other vehicles on all sides. I was freaking out." I admitted.

"The individual, you were told who he was. Is he in this room?"

"He is," I reply.

"Can you please point to him?"

And I do.

CHAPTER TWENTY-FOUR

BENJAMIN

THE CASE WAS CUT AND DRY.

Elliot's attorney tried to defend his client by arguing the vehicle he was driving had a malfunction. However, the district attorneys had an investigation launched on damages to the vehicle and there were no issues with the vehicle aside from the damage the crash caused, thereby refuting the argument.

The ruling was first degree attempted murder with a life sentence with a chance of parole.

With Elliot's one choice to cause harm, he ruined his life. While I should mourn the fact that my one-time close friend could do such a thing, I feel nothing. I feel relief that Bella survived, but I feel nothing about his punishment aside from satisfaction.

When the bailiff hauled a shut-down Elliot out of the court-room, he didn't fight it. He slowly stood and was lead out of the room in silence. He did, however, stop and finally look me in the eyes. His features portrayed a man lost, and for that I wished things could have been different.

In a different world, my parents would have never passed

away. Elliot and I would have started our company, and I would be married to Renae. She would have never felt ignored, never felt the need to run into another man's arms, so she would not have been in that fatal car accident.

But then again, I am finally happy with my world as it actually is, and I don't want that what-could-have-been world. Sure, it would be great to have my parents alive, but while I mourn the tragedies that pushed me to where I am not, I am grateful for the life I'm currently living

I have Bella.

I have an outstanding business.

The events of my past brought me to where I am today.

When Bella first came to work for me, I wasn't living. I was just working; I was a drone. I was like a dying flower, but she repotted me, fed me and made me better than I was before.

Bella renewed me.

EPILOGUE

The employees of Adams Enterprises no longer cower when I walk through the offices now. For some reason, they greet me with smiles and don't scatter anytime that I am near. It's taken some getting used to, but I find that I rather like it.

Some of the upper management employees I do business with nonchalantly poke around trying to figure out why I've changed so much in the past year. I'm not sure if they are aware or have figured out the source of my joy is the beautiful woman who keeps me on top of my shit, in and out of the office.

The accident was horrific but we've moved on. My thoughts of losing her that day made it absolutely one of the worst days in recent years. Having to deal with the court stuff afterwards reopened wounds, but now we have moved on.

Bella has officially moved into my penthouse; however, she still insists on keeping our relationship out of the office. I have occasionally been successful at catching her in the mood and have managed to bend her over my desk or hers and take her from time to time. Each time, she tells me that it will be the last time. But we both know, that is a complete lie as we can't get enough of one another to go all day without some form of touching. We keep everything private and no one in the company suspects our relationship.

The relationship contract is now being used consistently and the company has been successful in protecting assets. We haven't had any situation arise where any lawsuits could be filed, however Micah did get a divorce. And now, he's signed one of the contracts.

Today is the anniversary of our first date – the Gala – and I couldn't be more excited for her to see the dress I got her for this year's event this evening.

She's in the bedroom with the makeup artist and hair stylist and I'm pacing the hallway, waiting anxiously for her to come out. When she does, I smile. Her hair is half up and half down. Her hair is adorned with Swarovski Crystals around the bun in her hair. Her makeup is simple, only highlighting her cheekbones and her beautiful blue eyes.

"Where is this dress you've hidden from me?" she asks.

I smile and then lead her back into our bedroom, to the massive closet that houses a his and hers sides. It's big enough it could double as another bedroom.

I pull out the dress, covered by a garment bag and place it on the hook that I have sticking out of one of the cabinets. I slowly unzip the bag and then, before I unveil the dress, I ask her to turn around. When she complies, I remove the bag and puff out the dress fully.

I ask her to turn around and when she does, her hands fly to her mouth. Her eyes moisten as small whimper come out from behind her hand.

"Do you... Do you like it?" I ask her hesitantly, unsure if her reaction is of disgust or love. A moment passes before she removes her hands from her mouth. Tears are forming in her eyes, she places her hands over her heart and lets out a whimper.

"I love. I love it!" she says, rushing to the dress.

"Please. Put it on?" I beg of her.

She quickly disrobes and puts on her new dress purposely drawing out her movements to drive me crazy. She turns her back to me, so I can zip her up and then steps back to face me.

She looks amazing. My woman looks absolutely stunning.

The dress is gold, with yellow and white Swarovski crystals adorning the waist and some on the pleats of the dress. The fabric hangs off the shoulders and the bodice is fitted perfectly. The bottom half of the dress is a ball-gown with silk organza covering a lightweight white petticoat, which adds volume to the gown.

"It's beautiful, Ben. Absolutely beautiful. It looks like it would be so heavy to wear, but it's like I'm wearing air. It's magnificent."

"You, my love... You look beautiful."

"I feel like a princess!" she exclaims as she twirls.

Over the length of our relationship, we've teased ONE another with the nicknames of Beauty and the Beast. It's rung true from time to time, as I have been known to be a bit of a scary individual and she, well, she couldn't be more beautiful.

My Isabella, my Bella. My Beauty.

She is the beauty, to me – the beast.

Thank you for reading this fairytale re-telling. I hope you enjoyed it. Please share your thoughts on the book by Clicking here

READ MORE BY TARRAH ANDERS

THE NEIGHBORHOOD SERIES
THE MELTED SERIES
THE NIGHT MOVES SERIES
WHAT HAPPENS IN... SERIES

STANDALONES

New Year, New You

The Brute

Summer Fling

CLUTCH Endgame

Change of Scenery

More than Friends

No More Heartache

Fly Girl

Speakeasy (Storybook Pub Anthology)

In the End (A Quarantine Romance)

Rookie Moves (A Quick Snap Novella)

Love Surreptitiously

Little White Lie

Love on the Sidelines (A Quick Snap Novella)

Heartburn (An Everyday Heroes World Novel)

Do you want more info about Tarrah Anders and her releases? Sign up for her VIP Newsletter today!

DEAR FRIENDS,

I hope that in some shape or form you felt connected to my characters, I strive to have my stories be as relatable as possible, and not too outrageous. The sole purpose for me to bring my friends these stories is to feel like that too can be you.

That being said, I write to make you happy. I wouldn't be able to do so without your feedback. Whether if you leave a review on your favorite book retail site (Please do that would be spectacular) or if you feel like shooting me a message at: tarrah.anders@gmail.com . I would love to hear from you.

Please check out my website at: WWW.TARRAHANDERS.COM

Smooches ~ Tarrah

ACKNOWLEDGMENTS

First and foremost, thank YOU to the readers, the bloggers, **THE** people. I write to entertain you for however long you deem to let my words into your mind. Thank you for picking up this little ditty and giving me a chance.

I thank my husband for putting up with my ignoring him and the kids at times to write, edit, market and daydream. Without you by my side, I'm not sure that I would be so grounded. You are my rock. Thank you for your support and thank you for giving me eye candy when you get out of the shower.

Thanks to Jess Bryant and Maren Lee for your constant cheerleading. You two are two of the most amazing chicks that I've had the opportunity to share my authoring journey on. I'm so fortunate to have crossed paths with each of you.

To *The Teases*, my street team: Thank you for pimping me out on social media, for reading and reviewing and your overall support.

To the ladies of the Tarrah's Teases, my reader group. Thank you for your continued support and devotion.

To my betas Tamera & Mel. Thank you for the gushing, the critique and the overall awesomeness that you guys are!

To Laura, of Red Pen Princess. Your amazing editing skills are top notch. Thank you for editing, reading and loving me despite my punctuation and my lack of use of ONE another. Also, for the awesome facts when I misrepresent a word. You are a cave of wisdom.

Tarrah Anders is a contemporary romance author who is all about the feels, with the twists of sexy mixed in between. Writing has always been a passion and Tarrah loves to share her words, her characters and the world that they live in with her readers. Tarrah enjoys creating characters that you can be friends with, so get ready to make some new friends.

She is originally from the San Francisco Bay Area, but living in beautiful San Diego with her family, while working in Program Management within the social work field.

Printed in Great Britain
by Amazon